A CHRISTMAS CAROL

小氣財神

原著雙語彩圖本

作者——
狄更斯
（Charles Dickens）

譯者——
楊舒評

Contents

A ★ CHRISTMAS ★ CAROL

小氣財神

A CHRISTMAS CAROL

Stave One

Marley's Ghost

Marley was dead, to begin with. There is no doubt whatever about that. The register of his burial was signed by the clergyman, the clerk, the undertaker, and the chief mourner. Scrooge signed it. And Scrooge's name was good upon 'Change[1] for anything he chose to put his hand to.

Old Marley was as dead as a door-nail[2].

Mind! I don't mean to say that I know of my own knowledge, what there is particularly dead about a door-nail. I might have been inclined, myself, to regard a coffin-nail as the deadest piece of ironmongery in the trade. But the wisdom of our ancestors is in the simile; and my unhallowed hands shall not disturb it, or the country's done for. You will, therefore, permit

---

1　指當時倫敦的皇家交易所（Royal Exchange）。
2　「as dead as a doornail」是莎士比亞時代常見的譬喻法。

me to repeat, emphatically, that Marley was as dead as a door-nail.

Ebenezer Scrooge

Scrooge knew he was dead? Of course he did. How could it be otherwise? Scrooge and he were partners for I don't know how many years. Scrooge was his sole executor, his sole administrator, his sole assign, his sole residuary legatee, his sole friend, and sole mourner. And even Scrooge was not so dreadfully cut up by the sad event but that he was an excellent man of business on the very day of the funeral, and solemnised it with an undoubted bargain.

The mention of Marley's funeral brings me back to the point I started from. There is no doubt that Marley was dead. This must be distinctly understood, or nothing wonderful can come of the story I am going to relate. If we were not perfectly convinced that Hamlet's father died before the play began, there would be nothing more remarkable in his taking a stroll at night, in an easterly wind, upon his own ramparts, than there would be in any other middle-aged gentleman rashly turning out after dark in a breezy spot—say St. Paul's Churchyard for instance—literally to astonish his son's weak mind.

Scrooge never painted out Old Marley's name. There it stood, years afterwards, above the warehouse door: Scrooge and Marley. The firm was known as Scrooge and Marley. Sometimes people new to the business called Scrooge Scrooge, and sometimes Marley, but he answered to both names. It was all the same to him.

Oh! but he was a tight-fisted hand at the grindstone, Scrooge! a squeezing, wrenching, grasping, scraping, clutching, covetous old sinner! Hard and sharp as flint, from which no steel had ever struck out generous fire; secret, and self-contained, and solitary as an oyster. The cold within him froze his old features, nipped his pointed nose, shrivelled his cheek, stiffened his gait; made his eyes red, his thin lips blue; and spoke out shrewdly in his grating voice. A frosty rime was on his head, and on his eyebrows, and his wiry chin. He carried his own low temperature always about with him; he iced his office in the dog-days, and didn't thaw it one degree at Christmas.

External heat and cold had little influence on

Scrooge. No warmth could warm, nor wintry weather chill him. No wind that blew was bitterer than he, no falling snow was more intent upon its purpose, no pelting rain less open to entreaty. Foul weather didn't know where to have him. The heaviest rain, and snow, and hail, and sleet, could boast of the advantage over him in only one respect. They often "came down" handsomely, and Scrooge never did.

Nobody ever stopped him in the street to say, with gladsome looks, "My dear Scrooge, how are you? When will you come to see me?" No beggars implored him

No beggars implored him to bestow a trifle.

to bestow a trifle, no children asked him what it was o'clock, no man or woman ever once in all his life inquired the way to such and such a place, of Scrooge. Even the blind men's dogs appeared to know him; and, when they saw him coming on, would tug their owners into doorways and up courts; and then would wag their tails as though they said, "No eye at all is better than an evil eye, dark master!"

But what did Scrooge care? It was the very thing he liked. To edge his way along the crowded paths of life, warning all human sympathy to keep its distance, was what the knowing ones call "nuts" to Scrooge.

Once upon a time—of all the good days in the year, on Christmas Eve—old Scrooge sat busy in his counting-house. It was cold, bleak, biting weather; foggy withal; and he could hear the people in the court outside go wheezing up and down, beating their hands upon their breasts, and stamping their feet upon the pavement-stones to warm them. The City clocks had only just gone three, but it was quite dark already—it had not been light all day—and candles were flaring in the windows of the neighbouring offices, like ruddy smears upon the palpable brown air. The fog came pouring in at every chink and keyhole, and was so dense without,

Old Scrooge sat busy in his counting-house.

Wherefore the clerk put on his white comforter,
and tried to warm himself at the candle.

that, although the court was of the narrowest, the houses opposite were mere phantoms. To see the dingy cloud come drooping down, obscuring everything, one might have thought that nature lived hard by, and was brewing on a large scale.

The door of Scrooge's counting-house was open, that he might keep his eye upon his clerk, who in a dismal little cell beyond, a sort of tank, was copying letters. Scrooge had a very small fire, but the clerk's fire was so very much smaller that it looked like one coal. But he couldn't replenish it, for Scrooge kept the coal-box in his own room; and so surely as the clerk came in with the shovel, the master predicted that it would be necessary for them to part. Wherefore the clerk put on his white comforter, and tried to warm himself at the candle; in which effort, not being a man of a strong imagination, he failed.

"A merry Christmas, uncle! God save you!" cried a cheerful voice. It was the voice of Scrooge's nephew, who came upon him so quickly that this was the first intimation he had of his approach.

"Bah!" said Scrooge, "Humbug!"

He had so heated himself with rapid walking in the fog and frost, this nephew of Scrooge's, that he was all

"A merry Christmas, uncle! God save you!"
cried a cheerful voice.

in a glow; his face was ruddy and handsome; his eyes sparkled, and his breath smoked again.

"Christmas a humbug, uncle!" said Scrooge's nephew. "You don't mean that, I am sure?"

"I do," said Scrooge. "Merry Christmas! What right have you to be merry? What reason have you to be merry? You're poor enough."

"Come, then," returned the nephew gaily. "What right have you to be dismal? What reason have you to be morose? You're rich enough."

Scrooge, having no better answer ready on the spur of the moment, said, "Bah!" again; and followed it up with "Humbug!"

"Don't be cross, uncle," said the nephew.

"What else can I be," returned the uncle, "when I live in such a world of fools as this? Merry Christmas! Out upon merry Christmas! What's Christmas time to you but a time for paying bills without money; a time for finding yourself a year older, but not an hour richer; a time for balancing your books, and having every item in 'em through a round dozen of months presented dead against you? If I could work my will," said Scrooge, indignantly, "every idiot who goes about with 'Merry Christmas' on his lips should be boiled with his own pudding, and buried with a stake of holly through his heart. He should!"

"Uncle!" pleaded the nephew.

"Nephew!" returned the uncle, sternly, "keep Christmas in your own way, and let me keep it in mine."

"Keep it!" repeated Scrooge's nephew. "But you don't keep it."

"Let me leave it alone, then," said Scrooge. "Much good may it do you! Much good it has ever done you!"

"There are many things from which I might have derived good, by which I have not profited, I dare say," returned the nephew; "Christmas among the rest. But I am sure I have always thought of Christmas-time, when it has come round—apart from the veneration due to its sacred name and origin, if anything belonging to it can be apart from that—as a good time; a kind, forgiving, charitable, pleasant time; the only time I know of, in the long calendar of the year, when men and women seem by one consent to open their shut-up hearts freely, and to think of people below them as if they really were fellow-passengers to the grave, and not another race of creatures bound on other journeys. And therefore, uncle, though it

"Let me leave it alone, then," said Scrooge.

has never put a scrap of gold or silver in my pocket, I believe that it *has* done me good, and *will* do me good; and I say, God bless it!"

The clerk in the tank involuntarily applauded. Becoming immediately sensible of the impropriety, he poked the fire, and extinguished the last frail spark for ever.

"Let me hear another sound from *you*," said Scrooge, "and you'll keep your Christmas by losing your situation! You're quite a powerful speaker, sir," he added, turning to his nephew. "I wonder you don't go into Parliament."

"Don't be angry, uncle. Come! Dine with us tomorrow."

Scrooge said that he would see him[3] —Yes, indeed he did. He went the whole length of the expression, and said that he would see him in that extremity first.

"But why?" cried Scrooge's nephew. "Why?"

"Why did you get married[4]?" said Scrooge.

3　未講完的詛咒語，完整語為「see him go to the devil first」，指「想先看他去死」。

4　指外甥沒有錢，卻敢結婚；而為愛情結婚，更是荒謬。

"Because I fell in love."

"Because you fell in love!" growled Scrooge, as if that were the only one thing in the world more ridiculous than a merry Christmas. "Good afternoon!"

"Nay, uncle, but you never came to see me before that happened. Why give it as a reason for not coming now?"

"Good afternoon," said Scrooge.

"I want nothing from you; I ask nothing of you; why cannot we be friends?"

"Good afternoon," said Scrooge.

"I am sorry, with all my heart, to find you so resolute. We have never had any quarrel, to which I have been a party. But I have made the trial in homage to Christmas, and I'll keep my Christmas humour to the last. So a merry Christmas, uncle!"

"Good afternoon!" said Scrooge.

"And a happy New Year!"

"Good afternoon!" said Scrooge.

His nephew left the room without an angry word, notwithstanding. He stopped at the outer door to bestow the greetings of the season on the clerk, who, cold as he was, was warmer than Scrooge; for he returned them cordially.

"There's another fellow," muttered Scrooge; who overheard him: "my clerk, with fifteen shillings a-week, and a wife and family, talking about a merry Christmas. I'll retire to Bedlam."

This lunatic, in letting Scrooge's nephew out, had let two other people in. They were portly gentlemen, pleasant to behold, and now stood, with their hats off, in Scrooge's office. They had books and papers in their hands, and bowed to him.

"Scrooge and Marley's, I believe," said one of the gentlemen, referring to his list. "Have I the pleasure of addressing Mr. Scrooge, or Mr. Marley?"

"Mr. Marley has been dead these seven years," Scrooge replied. "He died seven years ago, this very night."

"We have no doubt his liberality is well represented by his surviving partner," said the gentleman, presenting his credentials.

It certainly was; for they had been two kindred spirits. At the ominous word "liberality" Scrooge frowned, and shook his head, and handed the credentials back.

"At this festive season of the year, Mr. Scrooge," said the gentleman, taking up a pen, "it is more than

"Have I the pleasure of addressing Mr. Scrooge,
or Mr. Marley?"

usually desirable that we should make some slight provision for the poor and destitute, who suffer greatly at the present time. Many thousands are in want of common necessaries; hundreds of thousands are in want of common comforts, sir."

"Are there no prisons?" asked Scrooge.

"Plenty of prisons," said the gentleman, laying down the pen again.

"And the Union workhouses[5]?" demanded Scrooge. "Are they still in operation?"

"They are. Still," returned the gentleman, "I wish I could say they were not."

"The Treadmill and the Poor Law[6] are in full vigour, then?" said Scrooge.

"Both very busy, sir."

"Oh! I was afraid, from what you said at first, that something had occurred to stop them in their useful course," said Scrooge. "I'm very glad to hear it."

"Under the impression that they scarcely furnish Christian cheer of mind or body to the multitude,"

5　勞動救濟院 (workhouse)，是為貧弱之人提供住處和生計的機構。

6　《磨坊法》(Treadmill) 是針對犯人，讓犯人踩踏車，有些並藉此產生動力，用來從事生產。《濟貧法》(Poor Law) 是用於勞動救濟院。

returned the gentleman, "a few of us are endeavouring to raise a fund to buy the Poor some meat and drink, and means of warmth. We choose this time because it is a time, of all others, when Want is keenly felt, and Abundance rejoices. What shall I put you down for?"

"Nothing!" Scrooge replied.

"You wish to be anonymous?"

"I wish to be left alone," said Scrooge. "Since you ask me what I wish, gentlemen, that is my answer. I don't make merry myself at Christmas, and I can't afford to make idle people merry. I help to support the establishments I have mentioned—they cost enough: and those who are badly off must go there."

"Many can't go there; and many would rather die."

"If they would rather die," said Scrooge, "they had better do it, and decrease the surplus population. Besides—excuse me—I don't know that."

"But you might know it," observed the gentleman.

"It's not my business," Scrooge returned. "It's enough for a man to understand his own business, and not to interfere with other people's. Mine occupies me constantly. Good afternoon, gentlemen!"

Seeing clearly that it would be useless to pursue their point, the gentlemen withdrew. Scrooge resumed his labours with an improved opinion of himself, and in a more facetious temper than was usual with him.

Meanwhile the fog and darkness thickened so, that people ran about with flaring links, proffering their services to go before horses in carriages, and conduct them on their way. The ancient tower of a church, whose gruff old bell was always peeping slily down at Scrooge out of a Gothic window in the wall, became invisible, and struck the hours and quarters in the clouds, with tremulous vibrations afterwards, as if its teeth were chattering in its frozen head up there.

The cold became intense. In the main street, at the corner of the court, some labourers were repairing the gas-pipes, and had lighted a great fire in a brazier, round which a party of ragged men and boys were gathered: warming their hands and winking their eyes before the blaze in rapture. The water-plug being left in solitude, its overflowings suddenly congealed, and turned to misanthropic ice. The brightness of the shops, where holly sprigs and berries crackled in the lamp heat of the windows, made pale faces ruddy as they passed. Poulterers' and grocers' trades became a splendid joke: a glorious pageant, with which it was next to impossible to believe that such dull principles as bargain and sale had anything to do. The Lord Mayor, in the stronghold of the mighty Mansion House, gave orders to his fifty cooks and butlers to keep Christmas as a Lord Mayor's household should; and even the little tailor, whom he had fined five shillings on the previous Monday for being drunk and blood thirsty in the streets, stirred up tomorrow's pudding in his garret, while his lean wife and the baby sallied out to buy the beef.

Foggier yet, and colder! Piercing, searching, biting cold. If the good St. Dunstan[7] had but nipped the Evil Spirit's nose with a touch of such weather as that, instead of using his familiar weapons, then indeed he would have roared to lusty purpose. The owner of one scant young nose, gnawed and mumbled by the hungry cold as bones are gnawed by dogs, stooped down at Scrooge's keyhole to regale him with a Christmas carol; but at the first sound of

"God bless you, merry gentleman!
May nothing you dismay!"

---

7 聖鄧斯坦（St. Dunstan），十世紀左右的人物，曾是一名鐵匠。一日，惡魔化身來誘惑他，但是被他識破，他拿起一個燒紅的鐵鉗，挾住惡魔的鼻子，惡魔痛得唉唉大叫。

Scrooge seized the ruler with such energy of action, that the singer fled in terror, leaving the keyhole to the fog and even more congenial frost.

At length the hour of shutting up the counting-house arrived. With an ill-will Scrooge dismounted from his stool, and tacitly admitted the fact to the expectant clerk in the tank, who instantly snuffed his candle out, and put on his hat.

"You'll want all day tomorrow, I suppose?" said Scrooge.

"If quite convenient, sir."

"It's not convenient," said Scrooge, "and it's not fair. If I was to stop half-a-crown for it, you'd think yourself ill used, I'll be bound?"

The clerk smiled faintly.

"And yet," said Scrooge, "you don't think *me* ill used, when I pay a day's wages for no work."

The clerk observed that it was only once a year.

"A poor excuse for picking a man's pocket every twenty-fifth of December!" said Scrooge, buttoning his great coat to the chin. "But I suppose you must have the whole day. Be here all the earlier next morning."

The clerk promised that he would; and Scrooge walked out with a growl. The office was closed in a

"It's not convenient," said Scrooge.

The clerk went down
a slide on Cornhill.

twinkling, and the clerk, with the long ends of his white comforter dangling below his waist (for he boasted no great coat), went down a slide on Cornhill, at the end of a lane of boys, twenty times, in honour of its being Christmas Eve, and then ran home to Camden Town as hard as he could pelt, to play at blindman's-buff.

Scrooge took his melancholy dinner in his usual melancholy tavern; and having read all the newspapers, and beguiled the rest of the evening with his banker's book, went home to bed. He lived in chambers which had once belonged to his deceased partner. They were a gloomy suite of rooms, in a lowering pile of building up a yard, where it had so little business to be, that one could scarcely help fancying it must have run there when it was a young house, playing at hide-and-seek with other houses, and have forgotten the way out again. It was old enough now, and dreary enough; for nobody lived in it but Scrooge, the other rooms being all let out as offices. The yard was so dark that even Scrooge, who knew its every stone, was fain to grope with his hands. The fog and frost so hung about the black old gateway of the house, that it seemed as if the Genius of the Weather sat in mournful meditation on the threshold.

Now, it is a fact that there was nothing at all particular about the knocker on the door, except that it was very large. It is also a fact that Scrooge had seen it, night and morning, during his whole residence in that place; also that Scrooge had as little of what is called fancy about him as any man in the City of London, even including—which is a bold word— the corporation, aldermen, and livery. Let it also be borne in mind that Scrooge had not bestowed one thought on Marley since his last mention of his seven-years'-dead partner that afternoon. And then let any man explain to me, if he can, how it happened that Scrooge, having his key in the lock of the door, saw in the knocker, without its undergoing any intermediate process of change—not a knocker, but Marley's face.

Marley's face. It was not in impenetrable shadow as the other objects in the yard were, but had a dismal light about it, like a bad lobster in a dark cellar. It was not angry or ferocious, but looked at Scrooge as Marley used to look; with ghostly spectacles turned up upon its ghostly forehead. The hair was curiously stirred, as if by breath or hot air; and, though the eyes were wide open, they were perfectly motionless. That, and its

Not a knocker, but Marley's face.

livid colour, made it horrible; but its horror seemed to be in spite of the face, and beyond its control, rather than a part of its own expression.

As Scrooge looked fixedly at this phenomenon, it was a knocker again.

To say that he was not startled, or that his blood was not conscious of a terrible sensation to which it had been a stranger from infancy, would be untrue. But he put his hand upon the key he had relinquished, turned it sturdily, walked in, and lighted his candle.

He *did* pause, with a moment's irresolution, before he shut the door; and he *did* look cautiously behind it first, as if he half expected to be terrified with the sight of Marley's pig tail sticking out into the hall. But there was nothing on the back of the door, except the screws and nuts that held the knocker on, so he said "Pooh, pooh!" and closed it with a bang.

The sound resounded through the house like thunder. Every room above, and every cask in the wine-merchant's cellars below, appeared to have a separate peal of echoes of its own. Scrooge was not a man to be frightened by echoes. He fastened the door, and walked across the hall, and up the stairs; slowly too: trimming his candle as he went.

You may talk vaguely about driving a coach and six up a good old flight of stairs, or through a bad young Act of Parliament[8]; but I mean to say you might have got a hearse up that staircase, and taken it broadwise, with the splinter-bar towards the wall, and the door towards the balustrades: and done it easy. There was plenty of width for that, and room to spare; which is perhaps the reason why Scrooge thought he saw a locomotive hearse going on before him in the gloom. Half-a-dozen gas-lamps out of the street wouldn't have lighted the entry too well, so you may suppose that it was pretty dark with Scrooge's dip.

Up Scrooge went, not caring a button for that. Darkness is cheap, and Scrooge liked it. But, before he shut his heavy door, he walked through his rooms to see that all was right. He had just enough recollection of the face to desire to do that.

Sitting-room, bedroom, lumber-room. All as they should be. Nobody under the table, nobody under the sofa; a small fire in the grate; spoon and basin ready; and the little saucepan of gruel (Scrooge had a cold

---

8 諷刺當時英國議會通過的法案往往漏洞百出，讓人能夠輕易地鑽法律漏洞。

in his head) upon the hob. Nobody under the bed; nobody in the closet; nobody in his dressing-gown, which was hanging up in a suspicious attitude against the wall. Lumber-room as usual. Old fire-guard, old shoes, two fish-baskets, washing-stand on three legs, and a poker.

Quite satisfied, he closed his door, and locked himself in; double locked himself in, which was not his custom. Thus secured against surprise, he took off his cravat; put on his dressing-gown and slippers, and his night-cap; and sat down before the fire to take his gruel.

It was a very low fire indeed; nothing on such a bitter night. He was obliged to sit close to it, and brood over it, before he could extract the least sensation of warmth from such a handful of fuel. The fireplace was an old one, built by some Dutch merchant long ago, and paved all round with quaint Dutch tiles, designed to illustrate the Scriptures. There were Cains and Abels, Pharaoh's daughters, Queens of Sheba, Angelic messengers descending through the air on clouds like feather-beds, Abrahams, Belshazzars, Apostles putting off to sea in butter-boats, hundreds of figures, to attract his thoughts; and yet that face of Marley, seven years dead, came like the ancient Prophet's rod, and swallowed up the whole[9]. If each smooth tile had been a blank at first, with power to shape some picture on its surface from the disjointed fragments of his thoughts, there would have been a copy of old Marley's head on every one.

"Humbug!" said Scrooge; and walked across the room.

After several turns, he sat down again. As he threw his head back in the chair, his glance happened to rest upon a bell, a disused bell, that hung in the room, and communicated, for some purpose now forgotten,

---

9　出自《舊約聖經・出埃及記》的典故：亞倫的手杖化成蛇，將其他人的手杖都吞噬掉。

with a chamber in the highest story of the building. It was with great astonishment, and with a strange, inexplicable dread, that as he looked, he saw this bell begin to swing. It swung so softly in the outset that it scarcely made a sound; but soon it rang out loudly, and so did every bell in the house.

This might have lasted half a minute, or a minute, but it seemed an hour. The bells ceased, as they had begun, together. They were succeeded by a clanking noise, deep down below as if some person were dragging a heavy chain over the casks in the wine-merchant's cellar. Scrooge then remembered to have heard that ghosts in haunted houses were described as dragging chains.

The cellar door flew open with a booming sound, and then he heard the noise much louder on the floors below; then coming up the stairs; then coming straight towards his door.

"It's humbug still!" said Scrooge. "I won't believe it."

His colour changed, though, when, without a pause, it came on through the heavy door, and passed into the room before his eyes. Upon its coming in, the dying flame leaped up, as though it cried, "I know him! Marley's Ghost!" and fell again.

It was with great astonishment, and with a strange, inexplicable
dread, that as he looked, he saw this bell begin to swing.

Upon its coming in, the dying flame leaped up, as though it cried, "I know him! Marley's Ghost!" and fell again.

The same face: the very same. Marley in his pig-tail, usual waistcoat, tights, and boots; the tassels on the latter bristling, like his pig tail, and his coat-skirts, and the hair upon his head. The chain he drew was clasped about his middle. It was long, and wound about him like a tail; and it was made (for Scrooge observed it closely) of cash-boxes, keys, padlocks, ledgers, deeds, and heavy purses wrought in steel. His body was transparent: so that Scrooge, observing him, and looking through his waistcoat, could see the two buttons on his coat behind.

Scrooge had often heard it said that Marley had no bowels, but he had never believed it until now.

No, nor did he believe it even now. Though he looked the phantom through and through, and saw it standing before him; though he felt the chilling influence of its death-cold eyes, and marked the very texture of the folded kerchief bound about its head and chin[10], which wrapper he had not observed before, he was still incredulous, and fought against his senses.

---

10 在狄更斯的時代，會用方巾從死者的頭頂繞到下巴綁住，以防下巴脫開。

"How now!" said Scrooge, caustic and cold as ever. "What do you want with me?"

"Much!"—Marley's voice; no doubt about it.

"Who are you?"

"Ask me who I *was*."

"Who *were* you, then?" said Scrooge, raising his voice. "You're particular, for a shade." He was going to say "*to a shade*," but substituted this, as more appropriate.

"In life I was your partner, Jacob Marley."

"Can you—can you sit down?" asked Scrooge, looking doubtfully at him.

"I can."

"Do it, then."

Scrooge asked the question, because he didn't know whether a ghost so transparent might find himself in a condition to take a chair; and felt that in the event of its being impossible, it might involve the necessity of an embarrassing explanation. But the Ghost sat down on the opposite side of the fireplace, as if he were quite used to it.

"You don't believe in me," observed the Ghost.

"I don't," said Scrooge.

"What evidence would you have of my reality, beyond that of your senses?"

"I don't know," said Scrooge.

"Why do you doubt your senses?"

"Because," said Scrooge, "a little thing affects them. A slight disorder of the stomach makes them cheats. You may be an undigested bit of beef, a blot of mustard, a crumb of cheese, a fragment of an underdone potato. There's more of gravy than of grave about you, whatever you are!"

Scrooge was not much in the habit of cracking jokes, nor did he feel, in his heart, by any means waggish then. The truth is, that he tried to be smart, as a means of distracting his own attention, and keeping down his terror; for the spectre's voice disturbed the very marrow in his bones.

To sit, staring at those fixed, glazed eyes, in silence, for a moment, would play, Scrooge felt, the very deuce with him. There was something very awful, too, in the spectre's being provided with an infernal atmosphere of his own. Scrooge could not feel it himself, but this was clearly the case; for though the Ghost sat perfectly motionless, its hair, and skirts, and tassels were still agitated as by the hot vapour from an oven.

"You see this toothpick?" said Scrooge, returning quickly to the charge, for the reason just assigned;

Marley's Ghost

and wishing, though it were only for a second, to divert the vision's stony gaze from himself.

"I do," replied the Ghost.

"You are not looking at it," said Scrooge.

"But I see it," said the Ghost, "notwithstanding."

"Well!" returned Scrooge, "I have but to swallow this, and be for the rest of my days persecuted by a legion of goblins, all of my own creation. Humbug, I tell you: humbug!"

At this, the spirit raised a frightful cry, and shook its chain with such a dismal and appalling noise, that Scrooge held on tight to his chair, to save himself from falling in a swoon. But how much greater was his horror when the phantom, taking off the bandage round its head, as if it were too warm to wear in-doors, its lower jaw dropped down upon its breast!

Scrooge fell upon his knees, and clasped his hands before his face.

"Mercy!" he said. "Dreadful apparition, why do you trouble me?"

"Man of the worldly mind!" replied the Ghost, "do you believe in me or not?"

"I do," said Scrooge; "I must. But why do spirits walk the earth, and why do they come to me?"

"It is required of every man," the Ghost returned, "that the spirit within him should walk abroad among his fellow-men, and travel far and wide; and, if that spirit goes not forth in life, it is condemned to do so after death. It is doomed to wander through the world—oh, woe is me!—and witness what it cannot share, but might have shared on earth, and turned to happiness!"

Again the spectre raised a cry, and shook its chain and wrung its shadowy hands.

"You are fettered," said Scrooge, trembling. "Tell me why?"

"I wear the chain I forged in life," replied the Ghost. "I made it link by link, and yard by yard; I girded it on of my own free will, and of my own free will I wore it. Is its pattern strange to *you*?"

Scrooge trembled more and more.

"Or would you know," pursued the Ghost, "the weight and length of the strong coil you bear yourself? It was full as heavy and as long as this, seven Christmas Eves ago. You have laboured on it since. It is a ponderous chain!"

Scrooge glanced about him on the floor, in the expectation of finding himself surrounded by some fifty or sixty fathoms of iron cable; but he could see nothing.

"Jacob," he said, imploringly. "Old Jacob Marley, tell me more! Speak comfort to me, Jacob."

"I have none to give," the Ghost replied. "It comes from other regions, Ebenezer Scrooge, and is conveyed by other ministers, to other kinds of men. Nor can I tell you what I would. A very little more is all permitted to me. I cannot rest, I cannot stay, I cannot linger anywhere. My spirit never walked beyond our counting-house—mark me;—in life my spirit never roved beyond the narrow limits of our money-changing hole; and weary journeys lie before me!"

It was a habit with Scrooge, whenever he became thoughtful, to put his hands in his breeches pockets. Pondering on what the Ghost had said, he did so now, but without lifting up his eyes, or getting off his knees.

"You must have been very slow about it, Jacob," Scrooge observed, in a business-like manner, though with humility and deference.

"Slow!" the Ghost repeated.

"Seven years dead," mused Scrooge. "And travelling all the time?"

On the wings of the wind

"The whole time," said the Ghost. "No rest, no peace. Incessant torture of remorse."

"You travel fast?" said Scrooge.

"On the wings of the wind," replied the Ghost.

"You might have got over a great quantity of ground in seven years," said Scrooge.

The Ghost, on hearing this, set up another cry, and clanked its chain so hideously in the dead silence of the night, that the Ward would have been justified in indicting it for a nuisance.

"Oh! captive, bound, and double-ironed," cried the phantom, "not to know, that ages of incessant labour by immortal creatures, for this earth must pass into eternity before the good of which it is susceptible is all developed! Not to know that any Christian spirit working kindly in its little sphere, whatever it may be, will find its mortal life too short for its vast means of usefulness! Not to know that no space of regret can make amends for one life's opportunity misused! Yet such was I! Oh! such was I!"

"But you were always a good man of business, Jacob," faltered Scrooge, who now began to apply this to himself.

"Business!" cried the Ghost, wringing its hands again. "Mankind was my business. The common welfare was my business; charity, mercy, forbearance, and benevolence, were, all, my business. The dealings of my trade were but a drop of water in the comprehensive ocean of my business!"

It held up its chain at arm's-length, as if that were

the cause of all its unavailing grief, and flung it heavily upon the ground again.

"At this time of the rolling year," the spectre said, "I suffer most. Why did I walk through crowds of fellow-beings with my eyes turned down, and never raise them to that blessed Star which led the Wise Men to a poor abode? Were there no poor homes to which its light would have conducted *me*!"

Scrooge was very much dismayed to hear the spectre going on at this rate, and began to quake exceedingly.

"Hear me!" cried the Ghost. "My time is nearly gone."

"I will," said Scrooge. "But don't be hard upon me! Don't be flowery, Jacob! Pray!"

"How it is that I appear before you in a shape that you can see, I may not tell. I have sat invisible beside you many and many a day."

It was not an agreeable idea. Scrooge shivered, and wiped the perspiration from his brow.

"That is no light part of my penance," pursued the Ghost. "I am here tonight to warn you that you have yet a chance and hope of escaping my fate. A chance and hope of my procuring, Ebenezer."

"You were always a good friend to me," said Scrooge. "Thank'ee!"

"You will be haunted," resumed the Ghost, "by Three Spirits."

Scrooge's countenance fell almost as low as the Ghost's had done.

"Is that the chance and hope you mentioned, Jacob?" he demanded, in a faultering voice.

"It is."

"I—I think I'd rather not," said Scrooge.

"Without their visits," said the Ghost, "you cannot hope to shun the path I tread. Expect the first tomorrow, when the bell tolls One."

"Couldn't I take 'em all at once, and have it over, Jacob?" hinted Scrooge.

"Expect the second on the next night at the same hour. The third upon the next night when the last stroke of Twelve has ceased to vibrate. Look to see me no more; and look that, for your own sake, you remember what has passed between us!"

When it had said these words, the spectre took its wrapper from the table, and bound it round its head as before. Scrooge knew this by the smart sound its teeth made when the jaws were brought together by the

"You will be haunted," resumed the Ghost,
"by Three Spirits."

bandage. He ventured to raise his eyes again, and found his supernatural visitor confronting him in an erect attitude, with its chain wound over and about its arm.

The apparition walked backward from him; and, at every step it took, the window raised itself a little, so that, when the spectre reached it, it was wide open. It beckoned Scrooge to approach, which he did. When they were within two paces of each other, Marley's Ghost held up its hand, warning him to come no nearer. Scrooge stopped.

Not so much in obedience, as in surprise and fear; for on the raising of the hand, he became sensible of confused noises in the air; incoherent sounds of lamentation and regret; wailings inexpressibly sorrowful and self-accusatory. The spectre, after listening for a moment, joined in the mournful dirge; and floated out upon the bleak, dark night.

Scrooge followed to the window: desperate in his curiosity. He looked out.

The air filled with phantoms, wandering hither and thither in restless haste, and moaning as they went. Every one of them wore chains like Marley's Ghost; some few (they might be guilty governments) were linked together; none were free.

Many had been personally known to Scrooge in their lives. He had been quite familiar with one old ghost in a white waistcoat, with a monstrous iron safe attached to its ankle, who cried piteously at being unable to assist a wretched woman with an infant, whom it saw below, upon a doorstep. The misery with them all was clearly, that they sought to interfere, for good, in human matters, and had lost the power for ever.

Whether these creatures faded into mist, or mist enshrouded them, he could not tell. But they and their spirit voices faded together; and the night became as it had been when he walked home.

Scrooge closed the window, and examined the door by which the Ghost had entered. It was double locked, as he had locked it with his own hands, and the bolts were undisturbed. He tried to say "Humbug!" but stopped at the first syllable. And being, from the emotion he had undergone, or the fatigues of the day, or his glimpse of the Invisible World, or the dull conversation of the Ghost, or the lateness of the hour, much in need of repose, went straight to bed, without undressing, and fell asleep upon the instant.

Stave Two

The First of the Three Spirits

When Scrooge awoke, it was so dark, that looking out of bed, he could scarcely distinguish the transparent window from the opaque walls of his chamber. He was endeavouring to pierce the darkness with his ferret eyes, when the chimes of a neighbouring church struck the four quarters. So he listened for the hour.

To his great astonishment, the heavy bell went on from six to seven, and from seven to eight, and regularly up to twelve; then stopped. Twelve! It was past two when he went to bed. The clock was wrong. An icicle must have got into the works. Twelve!

He touched the spring of his repeater, to correct this most preposterous clock. Its rapid little pulse beat twelve; and stopped.

"Why, it isn't possible," said Scrooge, "that I can have slept through a whole day and far into another night. It isn't possible that anything has happened to the sun, and this is twelve at noon!"

The idea being an alarming one, he scrambled out of bed, and groped his way to the window. He was obliged to rub the frost off with the sleeve of his dressing-gown before he could see anything; and could see very little then. All he could make out was, that it was still very foggy and extremely cold, and that there was no noise of people running to and fro, and making a great stir, as there unquestionably would have been if night had beaten off bright day, and taken possession of the world.

This was a great relief, because "three days after sight of this First of Exchange pay to Mr. Ebenezer Scrooge or his order," and so forth, would have become a mere United States' security if there were no days to count by.

Scrooge went to bed again, and thought, and thought, and thought it over and over, and could make nothing of it. The more he thought, the more perplexed he was; and the more he endeavoured not to think, the more he thought. Marley's Ghost bothered him exceedingly. Every time he resolved within himself, after mature inquiry, that it was all a dream, his mind flew back again, like a strong spring released, to its first position, and presented the same problem to be worked all through, "Was it a dream or not?"

Scrooge lay in this state until the chimes had gone three-quarters more, when he remembered, on a sudden, that the Ghost had warned him of a visitation when the bell tolled one. He resolved to lie awake until the hour was passed; and, considering that he could no more go to sleep than go to heaven, this was perhaps the wisest resolution in his power.

The quarter was so long, that he was more than once convinced he must have sunk into a doze unconsciously, and missed the clock. At length it broke upon his listening ear.

"Ding, dong!"

"A quarter past," said Scrooge, counting.

"Ding, dong!"

"Half past," said Scrooge.

"Ding, dong!"

"A quarter to it," said Scrooge.

"Ding, dong!"

"The hour itself," said Scrooge, triumphantly, "and nothing else!"

He spoke before the hour bell sounded, which it

now did with a deep,
dull, hollow, melancholy
ONE. Light flashed up
in the room upon the
instant, and the curtains
of his bed were drawn.

The curtains of his
bed were drawn aside, I
tell you, by a hand. Not
the curtains at his feet,
nor the curtains at his
back, but those to which
his face was addressed.
The curtains of his bed
were drawn aside; and
Scrooge, starting up
into a half-recumbent
attitude, found himself
face to face with the unearthly visitor who drew them:
as close to it as I am now to you, and I am standing in
the spirit at your elbow.

It was a strange figure—like a child: yet not so
like a child as like an old man, viewed through some
supernatural medium, which gave him the appearance

of having receded from the view, and being diminished to a child's proportions. Its hair, which hung about its neck and down its back, was white as if with age; and yet the face had not a wrinkle in it, and the tenderest bloom was on the skin. The arms were very long and muscular; the hands the same, as if its hold were of uncommon strength. Its legs and feet, most delicately formed, were, like those upper members, bare.

It wore a tunic of the purest white; and round its waist was bound a lustrous belt, the sheen of which was beautiful. It held a branch of fresh green holly in its hand; and, in singular contradiction of that wintry emblem, had its dress trimmed with summer flowers.

But the strangest thing about it was, that from the crown of its head there sprung a bright clear jet of light, by which all this was visible; and which was doubtless the occasion of its using, in its duller moments, a great extinguisher for a cap, which it now held under its arm.

Even this, though, when Scrooge looked at it with increasing steadiness, was *not* its strangest quality. For as its belt sparkled and glittered now in one part and now in another, and what was light one instant, at another time was dark, so the figure itself fluctuated in its distinctness; being now a thing with one arm, now with one leg, now with twenty legs, now a pair of legs without a head, now a head without a body: of which dissolving parts, no outline would be visible in the dense gloom wherein they melted away. And in the very wonder of this, it would be itself again; distinct and clear as ever.

"Are you the Spirit, sir, whose coming was foretold to me?" asked Scrooge.

"I am!"

The voice was soft and gentle. Singularly low, as if instead of being so close beside him, it were at a distance.

"Who, and what are you?" Scrooge demanded.

"I am the Ghost of Christmas Past."

"Long Past?" inquired Scrooge, observant of its dwarfish stature.

"No. Your past."

Perhaps, Scrooge could not have told anybody why, if anybody could have asked him; but he had a special desire to see the Spirit in his cap; and begged him to be covered.

"What!" exclaimed the Ghost, "would you so soon put out, with worldly hands, the light I give? Is it not enough that you are one of those whose passions

"Who, and what are you?" Scrooge demanded.
"I am the Ghost of Christmas Past."

made this cap, and force me through whole trains of years to wear it low upon my brow?"

Scrooge reverently disclaimed all intention to offend, or any knowledge of having wilfully "bonneted" the Spirit at any period of his life. He then made bold to inquire what business brought him there.

"Your welfare!" said the Ghost.

Scrooge expressed himself much obliged, but could not help thinking that a night of unbroken rest would have been more conducive to that end. The Spirit must have heard him thinking, for it said immediately:

"Your reclamation, then. Take heed!"

It put out its strong hand as it spoke, and clasped him gently by the arm.

"Rise! and walk with me!"

It would have been in vain for Scrooge to plead that the weather and the hour were not adapted to pedestrian purposes; that bed was warm, and the thermometer a long way below freezing; that he was clad but lightly in his slippers, dressing-gown, and nightcap; and that he had a cold upon him at that time. The grasp, though gentle as a woman's hand, was not to be resisted. He rose; but finding that the Spirit made towards the window, clasped its robe in supplication.

"I am a mortal," Scrooge remonstrated, "and liable to fall."

"Bear but a touch of my hand *there*," said the Spirit, laying it upon his heart, "and you shall be upheld in more than this!"

As the words were spoken, they passed through the wall, and stood upon an open country road, with fields on either hand. The city had entirely vanished. Not a vestige of it was to be seen. The darkness and the mist had vanished with it, for it was a clear, cold, winter day, with snow upon the ground.

"Good Heaven!" said Scrooge, clasping his hands together, as he looked about him. "I was bred in this place. I was a boy here!"

The Spirit gazed upon him mildly. Its gentle touch, though it had been light and instantaneous, appeared still present to the old man's sense of feeling. He was conscious of a thousand odours floating in the air, each one connected with a thousand thoughts, and hopes, and joys, and cares long, long, forgotten!

"Your lip is trembling," said the Ghost. "And what is that upon your cheek?"

Scrooge muttered, with an unusual catching in his

voice, that it was a pimple; and begged the Ghost to lead him where he would.

"You recollect the way?" inquired the Spirit.

"Remember it!" cried Scrooge with fervour—"I could walk it blindfold."

"Strange to have forgotten it for so many years!" observed the Ghost. "Let us go on."

They walked along the road; Scrooge recognising every gate, and post, and tree, until a little market-town appeared in the distance, with its bridge, its church, and winding river. Some shaggy ponies now were seen trotting towards them with boys upon their backs, who called to other boys in country gigs and carts, driven by farmers. All these boys were in great spirits, and shouted to each other, until the broad fields were so full of merry music, that the crisp air laughed to hear it.

"These are but shadows of the things that have been," said the Ghost. "They have no consciousness of us."

The jocund travellers came on; and as they came, Scrooge knew and named them every one. Why was he rejoiced beyond all bounds to see them? Why did his cold eye glisten, and his heart leap up as they went past? Why was he filled with gladness when he heard them give each other merry Christmas, as they parted at cross-roads and bye-ways, for their several homes? What was merry Christmas to Scrooge? Out upon merry Christmas! What good had it ever done to him?

"The school is not quite deserted," said the Ghost. "A solitary child, neglected by his friends, is left there still."

Scrooge said he knew it. And he sobbed.

They left the high-road by a well-remembered lane, and soon approached a mansion of dull red brick, with a little weather-cock surmounted cupola on the roof, and a bell hanging in it. It was a large house, but one of broken fortunes; for the spacious offices were little used, their walls were damp and mossy, their windows broken, and their gates decayed. Fowls clucked and strutted in the stables; and the coach-houses and sheds were over-run with grass.

Nor was it more retentive of its ancient state within; for entering the dreary hall, and glancing through the open doors of many rooms, they found them poorly furnished, cold, and vast. There was an earthy savour in the air, a chilly bareness in the place, which associated itself somehow with too much getting up

A lonely boy was reading near a feeble fire.

by candle-light, and not too much to eat.

They went, the Ghost and Scrooge, across the hall, to a door at the back of the house. It opened before them, and disclosed a long, bare, melancholy room, made barer still by lines of plain deal forms and desks. At one of these a lonely boy was reading near a feeble fire; and Scrooge sat down upon a form, and wept to see his poor forgotten self as he had used to be.

Not a latent echo in the house, not a squeak and scuffle from the mice behind the panelling, not a drip from the half-thawed water-spout in the dull yard behind, not a sigh among the leafless boughs of one despondent poplar, not the idle swinging of an empty store-house door, no, not a clicking in the fire, but fell upon the heart of Scrooge with a softening influence, and gave a freer passage to his tears.

The Spirit touched him on the arm, and pointed to his younger self, intent upon his reading. Suddenly a man, in foreign garments, wonderfully real and distinct to look at, stood outside the window, with an axe stuck in his belt, and leading an ass laden with wood by the bridle.

"Why, it's Ali Baba!" Scrooge exclaimed in ecstasy.

Scrooge sat down and wept to
see his poor forgotten self.

C.E.Brock
1905

"It's dear old honest Ali Baba! Yes, yes, I know. One Christmas time, when yonder solitary child was left here all alone, he *did* come, for the first time, just like that. Poor boy! And Valentine," said Scrooge, "and his wild brother, Orson; there they go! And what's his name, who was put down in his drawers, asleep, at the Gate of Damascus; don't you see him? And the Sultan's Groom turned upside down by the Genii; there he is upon his head! Serve him right! I'm glad of it. What business had he to be married to the Princess?"

To hear Scrooge expending all the earnestness of his nature on such subjects, in a most extraordinary voice between laughing and crying; and to see his heightened and excited face; would have been a surprise to his business friends in the city, indeed.

"There's the Parrot!" cried Scrooge. "Green body and yellow tail, with a thing like a lettuce growing out of the top of his head; there he is! Poor Robin Crusoe, he called him, when he came home again after sailing round the island. 'Poor Robin Crusoe, where have you been, Robin Crusoe?' The man thought he was dreaming, but he wasn't. It was the Parrot, you know. There goes Friday, running for his life to the little creek! Halloa! Hoop! Halloo!"

Then, with a rapidity of transition very foreign to his usual character, he said, in pity for his former self, "Poor boy!" and cried again.

"I wish," Scrooge muttered, putting his hand in his pocket, and looking about him, after drying his eyes with his cuff; "but it's too late now."

"What is the matter?" asked the Spirit.

"Nothing," said Scrooge. "Nothing. There was a boy singing a Christmas carol at my door last night. I should like to have given him something: that's all."

The Ghost smiled thoughtfully, and waved its hand, saying as it did so, "Let us see another Christmas!"

Scrooge's former self grew larger at the words, and the room became a little darker and more dirty. The panels shrunk, the windows cracked; fragments of plaster fell out of the ceiling, and the naked laths were shown instead; but how all this was brought about, Scrooge knew no more than you do. He only knew that it was quite correct; that everything had happened so; that there he was, alone again, when all the other boys had gone home for the jolly holidays.

He was not reading now, but walking up and down despairingly. Scrooge looked at the Ghost, and with a mournful shaking of his head, glanced anxiously towards the door.

It opened; and a little girl, much younger than the boy, came darting in, and putting her arms about his neck, and often kissing him, addressed him as her "dear, dear brother."

"I have come to bring you home, dear brother!" said the child, clapping her tiny hands, and bending down to laugh. "To bring you home, home, home!"

"Home, little Fan?" returned the boy.

"Yes!" said the child, brimful of glee. "Home, for good and all. Home, for ever and ever. Father is so much kinder than he used to be, that home's like heaven! He spoke so gently to me one dear night when I was going to bed, that I was not afraid to ask him once more if you might come home; and he said Yes, you should; and sent me in a coach to bring you. And you're to be a man!" said the child, opening her eyes; "and are never to come back here; but first, we're to be together all the Christmas long, and have the merriest time in all the world."

"You are quite a woman, little Fan!" exclaimed the boy.

She clapped her hands and laughed, and tried to touch his head; but being too little laughed again, and stood on tiptoe to embrace him. Then she began to drag him, in her childish eagerness, towards the door; and he, nothing loath to go, accompanied her.

A terrible voice in the hall cried, "Bring down Master Scrooge's box, there!" and in the hall appeared the schoolmaster himself, who glared on Master Scrooge with a ferocious condescension, and threw him into a dreadful state of mind by shaking hands with him.

He then conveyed him and his sister into the veriest old well of a shivering best parlour that ever was seen, where the maps upon the wall, and the celestial and terrestrial globes in the windows were waxy with cold. Here he produced a decanter of curiously light wine, and a block of curiously heavy cake, and administered instalments of those dainties to the young people; at the same time sending out a meagre servant to offer a glass of "something" to the postboy, who answered that he thanked the gentleman, but if it was the same tap as he had tasted before, he had rather not. Master Scrooge's trunk being by this time tied on to the top of the chaise, the children bade the schoolmaster good-bye right willingly; and getting into it, drove gaily down the garden sweep; the quick wheels dashing the hoar-frost and snow from off the dark leaves of the

Here he produced a decanter of curiously light wine,
and a block of curiously heavy cake.

evergreens like spray.

"Always a delicate creature, whom a breath might have withered," said the Ghost. "But she had a large heart!"

"So she had," cried Scrooge. "You're right. I'll not gainsay it, Spirit. God forbid!"

"She died a woman," said the Ghost, "and had, as I think, children."

"One child," Scrooge returned.

"True," said the Ghost. "Your nephew!"

Scrooge seemed uneasy in his mind, and answered briefly, "Yes."

Although they had but that moment left the school behind them, they were now in the busy thoroughfares of a city, where shadowy passengers passed and repassed; where shadowy carts and coaches battled for the way, and all the strife and tumult of a real city were. It was made plain enough, by the dressing of the shops, that here too it was Christmas time again; but it was evening, and the streets were lighted up.

The Ghost stopped at a certain warehouse door, and asked Scrooge if he knew it.

"Know it!" said Scrooge. "Was I apprenticed here?"

They went in. At sight of an old gentleman in a

Welsh wig, sitting behind such a high desk, that if he had been two inches taller he must have knocked his head against the ceiling, Scrooge cried in great excitement—

"Why, it's old Fezziwig! Bless his heart, it's Fezziwig alive again!"

Old Fezziwig laid down his pen, and looked up at the clock, which pointed to the hour of seven. He rubbed his hands; adjusted his capacious waistcoat; laughed all over himself, from his shoes to his organ of benevolence; and called out in a comfortable, oily, rich, fat, jovial voice—

"Yo ho, there! Ebenezer! Dick!"

Scrooge's former self, now grown a young man, came briskly in, accompanied by his fellow-'prentice.

"Dick Wilkins, to be sure!" said Scrooge to the Ghost. "Bless me, yes. There he is. He was very much attached to me, was Dick. Poor Dick! Dear, dear!"

"Yo ho, my boys!" said Fezziwig. "No more work tonight. Christmas Eve, Dick. Christmas, Ebenezer! Let's have the shutters up," cried old Fezziwig, with a sharp clap of his hands, "before a man can say, Jack Robinson!"

You wouldn't believe how those two fellows went

"Yo ho, my boys!" said Fezziwig.

at it! They charged into the street with the shutters—one, two, three—had 'em up in their places—four, five, six—barred 'em and pinned 'em—seven, eight, nine—and came back before you could have got to twelve, panting like race horses.

"Hilli-ho!" cried old Fezziwig, skipping down from the high desk with wonderful agility. "Clear away, my lads, and let's have lots of room here! Hilli-ho, Dick! Chirrup, Ebenezer!"

Clear away! There was nothing they wouldn't have cleared away, or couldn't have cleared away, with old Fezziwig looking on. It was done in a minute. Every movable was packed off, as if it were dismissed from public life for evermore; the floor was swept and watered, the lamps were trimmed, fuel was heaped upon the fire; and the warehouse was as snug, and warm, and dry, and bright a ball-room, as you would desire to see upon a winter's night.

In came a fiddler with a music-book, and went up to the lofty desk, and made an orchestra of it, and tuned like fifty stomach-aches. In came Mrs. Fezziwig, one vast substantial smile. In came the three Miss Fezziwigs, beaming and lovable. In came the six young followers whose hearts they broke. In came all the young men

In came a fiddler
with a music-book.

and women employed in the business. In came the
housemaid, with her cousin the baker. In came the cook
with her brother's particular friend the milkman. In
came the boy from over the way, who was suspected of
not having board enough from his master; trying to hide
himself behind the girl from next door but one, who
was proved to have had her ears pulled by her mistress.

In they all came, one after another; some shyly, some boldly, some gracefully, some awkwardly, some pushing, some pulling; in they all came, any how and every how. Away they all went, twenty couple at once; hands half round and back again the other way; down the middle and up again; round and round in various stages of affectionate grouping; old top couple always turning up in the wrong place; new top couple starting off again as soon as they got there; all top couples at last, and not a bottom one to help them.

When this result was brought about, old Fezziwig, clapping his hands to stop the dance, cried out, "Well done!" and the fiddler plunged his hot face into a pot of porter, especially provided for that purpose. But scorning rest upon his reappearance, he instantly began again, though there were no dancers yet, as if the other fiddler had been carried home, exhausted, on a shutter; and he were a bran-new man resolved to beat him out of sight, or perish.

There were more dances, and there were forfeits, and more dances, and there was cake, and there was negus, and there was a great piece of Cold Roast, and there was a great piece of Cold Boiled, and there were mince-pies, and plenty of beer. But the great effect of the evening came after the Roast and Boiled, when the fiddler (an artful dog, mind! The sort of man who knew his business better than you or I could have told it him!) struck up "Sir Roger de Coverley." Then old Fezziwig stood out to dance with Mrs. Fezziwig. Top couple, too; with a good stiff piece of work cut out for them; three or four and twenty pair of partners; people who were not to be trifled with; people who would dance, and had no notion of walking.

But if they had been twice as many—ah! four times—old Fezziwig would have been a match for them, and so would Mrs. Fezziwig. As to *her*, she was worthy to be his partner in every sense of the term. If that's not high praise, tell me higher, and I'll use it. A positive light appeared to issue from Fezziwig's calves. They shone in every part of the dance like moons. You couldn't have predicted, at any given time, what would become of them next.

And when old Fezziwig and Mrs. Fezziwig had gone all through the dance; advance and retire, hold hands with your partner; bow and curtsey; corkscrew; thread-the-needle, and back again to your place; Fezziwig "cut"—cut so deftly, that he appeared to wink with his legs, and came upon his feet again without a stagger.

Fezziwig stood out to dance with Mrs. Fezziwig.

When the clock struck eleven, this domestic ball broke up. Mr. and Mrs. Fezziwig took their stations, one on either side the door, and shaking hands with every person individually as he or she went out, wished him or her a merry Christmas. When everybody had retired but the two 'prentices, they did the same to them; and thus the cheerful voices died away, and the lads were left to their beds; which were under a counter in the back-shop.

During the whole of this time, Scrooge had acted like a man out of his wits. His heart and soul were in the scene, and with his former self. He corroborated everything, remembered everything, enjoyed everything, and underwent the strangest agitation. It was not until now, when the bright faces of his former self and Dick were turned from them, that he remembered the Ghost, and became conscious that it was looking full upon him, while the light upon its head burnt very clear.

"A small matter," said the Ghost, "to make these silly folks so full of gratitude."

"Small!" echoed Scrooge.

The Spirit signed to him to listen to the two apprentices, who were pouring out their hearts in praise of Fezziwig: and when he had done so, said,

"Why! Is it not? He has spent but a few pounds of your mortal money: three or four, perhaps. Is that so much that he deserves this praise?"

"It isn't that," said Scrooge, heated by the remark, and speaking unconsciously like his former, not his latter self. "It isn't that, Spirit. He has the power to render us happy or unhappy; to make our service light or burdensome; a pleasure or a toil. Say that his power lies in words and looks; in things so slight and insignificant that it is impossible to add and count 'em up: what then? The happiness he gives, is quite as great as if it cost a fortune."

He felt the Spirit's glance, and stopped.

"What is the matter?" asked the Ghost.

"Nothing particular," said Scrooge.

"Something, I think?" the Ghost insisted.

"No," said Scrooge, "no. I should like to be able to say a word or two to my clerk just now! That's all."

His former self turned down the lamps as he gave utterance to the wish; and Scrooge and the Ghost again stood side by side in the open air.

"My time grows short," observed the Spirit. "Quick!"

This was not addressed to Scrooge, or to any one whom he could see, but it produced an immediate effect. For again Scrooge saw himself. He was older now; a man in the prime of life. His face had not the harsh and rigid lines of later years; but it had begun to wear the signs of care and avarice. There was an eager, greedy, restless motion in the eye, which showed the passion that had taken root, and where the shadow of the growing tree would fall.

He was not alone, but sat by the side of a fair young girl in a mourning dress: in whose eyes there were tears, which sparkled in the light that shone out of the Ghost of Christmas Past.

"It matters little," she said, softly. "To you, very little. Another idol has displaced me; and if it can cheer and comfort you in time to come, as I would have tried to do, I have no just cause to grieve."

"What Idol has displaced you?" he rejoined.

"A golden one."

"This is the even-handed dealing of the world!" he said. "There is nothing on which it is so hard as poverty; and there is nothing it professes to condemn with such severity as the pursuit of wealth!"

"You fear the world too much," she answered gently. "All your other hopes have merged into the hope of being beyond the chance of its sordid reproach. I have seen your nobler aspirations fall off one by one, until the master passion, Gain, engrosses you. Have I not?"

"What then?" he retorted. "Even if I have grown so much wiser, what then? I am not changed towards you."

She shook her head.

"Am I?"

"Our contract is an old one. It was made when we were both poor and content to be so, until, in good season, we could improve our worldly fortune by our patient industry. You *are* changed. When it was made, you were another man."

"I was a boy," he said impatiently.

"Your own feeling tells you that you were not what you are," she returned. "I am. That which promised happiness when we were one in heart is fraught with misery now that we are two. How often and how keenly I have thought of this, I will not say. It is enough that I *have* thought of it, and can release you."

"Have I ever sought release?"

"In words. No. Never."

"In what, then?"

"In a changed nature; in an altered spirit; in another atmosphere of life; another Hope as its great end. In everything that made my love of any worth or value in your sight. If this had never been between us," said the girl, looking mildly, but with steadiness, upon him; "tell me, would you seek me out and try to win me now? Ah, no!"

He seemed to yield to the justice of this supposition, in spite of himself. But he said, with a struggle, "You think not."

"I would gladly think otherwise if I could," she answered, "Heaven knows! When *I* have learned a Truth like this, I know how strong and irresistible it must be. But if you were free today, tomorrow, yesterday, can even I believe that you would choose a dowerless girl—you who, in your very confidence with her, weigh everything by Gain: or, choosing her, if for a moment you were false enough to your one guiding principle to do so, do I not know that your repentance and regret would surely follow? I do; and I release you. With a full heart, for the love of him you once were."

He was about to speak; but with her head turned from him, she resumed.

"You may—the memory of what is past half makes me hope you will—have pain in this. A very, very brief time, and you will dismiss the recollection of it, gladly, as an unprofitable dream, from which it happened

I release you. With a full heart,
for the love of him you once were.

May you be happy in the life you have chosen!

well that you awoke. May you be happy in the life you have chosen!"

She left him; and they parted.

"Spirit!" said Scrooge, "show me no more! Conduct me home. Why do you delight to torture me?"

"One shadow more!" exclaimed the Ghost.

"No more!" cried Scrooge. "No more. I don't wish to see it. Show me no more!"

But the relentless Ghost pinioned him in both his arms, and forced him to observe what happened next.

They were in another scene and place: a room, not very large or handsome, but full of comfort. Near to the winter fire sat a beautiful young girl, so like the last that Scrooge believed it was the same, until he saw *her*, now a comely matron, sitting opposite her daughter. The noise in this room was perfectly tumultuous, for there were more children there than Scrooge in his agitated state of mind could count; and, unlike the celebrated herd in the poem[1], they were not forty children conducting themselves like one, but every child was conducting itself like forty.

---

1 指英國浪漫主義詩人華茲渥斯（William Wordsworth）的詩《寫於三月》（*Written in March*），其中一句寫道：「牛群埋頭吃草，四十隻牛每隻看起來都一樣。」（The cattle are grazing, Their heads never raising; There are forty feeding like one!）

The consequences were uproarious beyond belief; but no one seemed to care; on the contrary, the mother and daughter laughed heartily, and enjoyed it very much; and the latter, soon beginning to mingle in the sports, got pillaged by the young brigands most ruthlessly.

What would I not have given to be one of them! Though I never could have been so rude, no, no! I wouldn't for the wealth of all the world have crushed that braided hair, and torn it down; and for the precious little shoe, I wouldn't have plucked it off, God bless my soul! to save my life. As to measuring her waist in sport, as they did, bold young brood, I couldn't have done it; I should have expected my arm to have grown round it for a punishment, and never come straight again.

And yet I should have dearly liked, I own, to have touched her lips; to have questioned her, that she might have opened them; to have looked upon the lashes of her downcast eyes, and never raised a blush; to have let loose waves of hair, an inch of which would be a keepsake beyond price: in short, I should have liked, I do confess, to have had the lightest licence of a child, and yet been man enough to know its value.

But now a knocking at the door was heard, and such a rush immediately ensued that she with laughing face and plundered dress was borne towards it the centre of a flushed and boisterous group, just in time to greet the father, who came home attended by a man laden with Christmas toys and presents. Then the shouting and the struggling, and the onslaught that was made on the defenceless porter! The scaling him with chairs for ladders, to dive into his pockets, despoil him of brown-paper parcels, hold on tight by his cravat, hug him round the neck, pummel his back, and kick his legs in irrepressible affection! The shouts of wonder and delight with which the development of every package was received!

The terrible announcement that the baby had been taken in the act of putting a doll's frying-pan into his mouth, and was more than suspected of having swallowed a fictitious turkey, glued on a wooden platter! The immense relief of finding this a false alarm! The joy, and gratitude, and ecstasy! They are all indescribable alike. It is enough that by degrees the children and their emotions got out of the parlour and by one stair at a time, up to the top of the house; where they went to bed, and so subsided.

A flushed and boisterous group.

And now Scrooge looked on more attentively than ever, when the master of the house, having his daughter leaning fondly on him, sat down with her and her mother at his own fireside; and when he thought that such another creature, quite as graceful and as full of promise, might have called him father, and been a spring-time in the haggard winter of his life, his sight grew very dim indeed.

"Belle," said the husband, turning to his wife with a smile, "I saw an old friend of yours this afternoon."

"Who was it?"

"Guess!"

"How can I? Tut, don't I know?" she added in the same breath, laughing as he laughed. "Mr. Scrooge."

"Mr. Scrooge it was. I passed his office window; and as it was not shut up, and he had a candle inside, I could scarcely help seeing him. His partner lies upon the point of death, I hear; and there he sat alone. Quite alone in the world, I do believe."

"Spirit!" said Scrooge in a broken voice, "remove me from this place."

"I told you these were shadows of the things that have been," said the Ghost. "That they are what they are, do not blame me!"

Laden with Christmas toys and presents.

"Remove me!" Scrooge exclaimed, "I cannot bear it!"

He turned upon the Ghost, and seeing that it looked upon him with a face, in which in some strange way there were fragments of all the faces it had shown him, wrestled with it.

"Leave me! Take me back. Haunt me no longer!"

In the struggle, if that can be called a struggle in which the Ghost with no visible resistance on its own part was undisturbed by any effort of its adversary, Scrooge observed that its light was burning high and bright; and dimly connecting that with its influence over him, he seized the extinguisher-cap, and by a sudden action pressed it down upon its head.

The Spirit dropped beneath it, so that the extinguisher covered its whole form; but though Scrooge pressed it down with all his force, he could not hide the light, which streamed from under it, in an unbroken flood upon the ground.

He was conscious of being exhausted, and overcome by an irresistible drowsiness; and, further, of being in his own bedroom. He gave the cap a parting squeeze, in which his hand relaxed; and had barely time to reel to bed, before he sank into a heavy sleep.

Stave Three

The Second of the Three Spirits

Awaking in the middle of a prodigiously tough snore, and sitting up in bed to get his thoughts together, Scrooge had no occasion to be told that the bell was again upon the stroke of One. He felt that he was restored to consciousness in the right nick of time, for the especial purpose of holding a conference with the second messenger despatched to him through Jacob Marley's intervention. But, finding that he turned uncomfortably cold when he began to wonder which of his curtains this new spectre would draw back, he put them every one aside with his own hands; and lying down again, established a sharp look-out all round the bed. For he wished to challenge the Spirit on the moment of its appearance, and did not wish to be taken by surprise and made nervous.

"The bell was again upon the stroke of one."

Gentlemen of the free-and-easy sort, who plume themselves on being acquainted with a move or two, and being usually equal to the time-of-day, express the wide range of their capacity for adventure by observing that they are good for anything from pitch-and-toss to manslaughter; between which opposite extremes, no doubt, there lies a tolerably wide and comprehensive range of subjects. Without venturing for Scrooge quite as hardily as this, I don't mind calling on you to believe that he was ready for a good broad field of strange appearances, and that nothing between a baby and a rhinoceros would have astonished him very much.

Now, being prepared for almost anything, he was not by any means prepared for nothing; and, consequently, when the bell struck One, and no shape appeared, he was taken with a violent fit of trembling. Five minutes, ten minutes, a quarter of an hour went by, yet nothing came.

All this time, he lay upon his bed, the very core and centre of a blaze of ruddy light, which streamed upon it when the clock proclaimed the hour; and which being only light, was more alarming than a dozen ghosts, as he was powerless to make out what it meant, or would be at; and was sometimes apprehensive that he might be at that very moment an interesting case of spontaneous combustion, without having the consolation of knowing it.

At last, however, he began to think—as you or I would have thought at first; for it is always the person not in the predicament who knows what ought to have been done in it, and would unquestionably have done it too—at last, I say, he began to think that the source and secret of this ghostly light might be in the adjoining room: from whence, on further tracing it, it seemed to shine. This idea taking full possession of his mind, he got up softly and shuffled in his slippers to the door.

The moment Scrooge's hand was on the lock, a strange voice called him by his name, and bade him enter. He obeyed.

It was his own room. There was no doubt about that. But it had undergone a surprising transformation. The walls and ceiling were so hung with living green, that it looked a perfect grove, from every part of which, bright gleaming berries glistened. The crisp leaves of holly, mistletoe, and ivy reflected back the light, as if so many little mirrors had been scattered there; and such a mighty blaze went roaring up the chimney, as that dull petrification of a hearth had never known in Scrooge's time, or Marley's, or for many and many a winter season gone.

Heaped up on the floor, to form a kind of throne, were turkeys, geese, game, poultry, brawn, great joints of meat, sucking-pigs, long wreaths of sausages, mince-pies, plum-puddings, barrels of oysters, red-hot chestnuts, cherry-cheeked apples, juicy oranges, luscious pears, immense twelfth-cakes, and seething bowls of punch, that made the chamber dim with their delicious steam.

In easy state upon this couch, there sat a jolly Giant, glorious to see; who bore a glowing torch, in shape not unlike Plenty's horn, and held it up, high up, to shed its light on Scrooge, as he came peeping round the door.

"Come in!" exclaimed the Ghost. "Come in! and know me better, man!"

Scrooge entered timidly, and hung his head before this Spirit. He was not the dogged Scrooge he had been; and though the Spirit's eyes were clear and kind, he did not like to meet them.

"I am the Ghost of Christmas Present," said the

"I am the Ghost of Christmas Present,"
said the Spirit. "Look upon me!"

Spirit. "Look upon me!"

Scrooge reverently did so. It was clothed in one simple deep green robe, or mantle, bordered with white fur. This garment hung so loosely on the figure, that its capacious breast was bare, as if disdaining to be warded or concealed by any artifice. Its feet, observable beneath the ample folds of the garment, were also bare; and on its head it wore no other covering than a holly wreath, set here and there with shining icicles. Its dark brown curls were long and free; free as its genial face, its sparkling eye, its open hand, its cheery voice, its unconstrained demeanour, and its joyful air. Girded round its middle was an antique scabbard; but no sword was in it, and the ancient sheath was eaten up with rust.

"You have never seen the like of me before!" exclaimed the Spirit.

"Never," Scrooge made answer to it.

"Have never walked forth with the younger members of my family; meaning (for I am very young) my elder brothers born in these later years?" pursued the Phantom.

"I don't think I have," said Scrooge. "I am afraid I have not. Have you had many brothers, Spirit?"

"More than eighteen hundred," said the Ghost.

"A tremendous family to provide for," muttered Scrooge.

The Ghost of Christmas Present rose.

"Spirit," said Scrooge submissively, "conduct me where you will. I went forth last night on compulsion, and I learned a lesson which is working now. Tonight, if you have aught to teach me, let me profit by it."

"Touch my robe!"

Scrooge did as he was told, and held it fast.

Holly, mistletoe, red berries, ivy, turkeys, geese, game, poultry, brawn, meat, pigs, sausages, oysters, pies, puddings, fruit, and punch, all vanished instantly. So did the room, the fire, the ruddy glow, the hour of night, and they stood in the city streets on Christmas morning, where (for the weather was severe) the people made a rough, but brisk and not unpleasant kind of music, in scraping the snow from the pavement in front of their dwellings, and from the tops of their houses, whence it was mad delight to the boys to see it come plumping down into the road below, and splitting into artificial little snowstorms.

The house fronts looked black enough, and the windows blacker, contrasting with the smooth white sheet of snow upon the roofs, and with the dirtier snow upon the ground; which last deposit had been ploughed up in deep furrows by the heavy wheels of carts and waggons; furrows that crossed and re-crossed each other hundreds of times where the great streets branched off, and made intricate channels, hard to trace, in the thick yellow mud and icy water.

The sky was gloomy, and the shortest streets were choked up with a dingy mist, half thawed, half frozen, whose heavier particles descended in a shower of sooty atoms, as if all the chimneys in Great Britain had, by one consent, caught fire, and were blazing away to their dear hearts' content. There was nothing very cheerful in the climate or the town, and yet was there an air of cheerfulness abroad that the clearest summer air and brightest summer sun might have endeavoured to diffuse in vain.

For the people who were shovelling away on the housetops were jovial and full of glee; calling out to one another from the parapets, and now and then exchanging a facetious snowball—better-natured missile far than many a wordy jest—laughing heartily if it went right, and not less heartily if it went wrong.

There was nothing very cheerful in the climate

The poulterers' shops were still half open, and the fruiterers' were radiant in their glory.

There were great round, pot-bellied baskets of chestnuts, shaped like the waistcoats of jolly old gentlemen, lolling at the doors, and tumbling out into the street in their apoplectic opulence.

There were ruddy, brown-faced, broad-girthed Spanish onions, shining in the fatness of their growth like Spanish friars, and winking from their shelves in wanton slyness at the girls as they went by, and glanced demurely at the hung-up mistletoe.

There were pears and apples clustered high in blooming pyramids; there were bunches of grapes, made in the shopkeepers' benevolence to dangle from conspicuous hooks, that people's mouths might water gratis as they passed; there were piles of filberts, mossy and brown, recalling, in their fragrance, ancient walks among the woods, and pleasant shufflings ankle deep through withered leaves; there were Norfolk Biffins, squab and swarthy, setting off the yellow of the oranges and lemons, and, in the great compactness of their juicy persons, urgently entreating and beseeching to be carried home in paper bags and eaten after dinner.

The very gold and silver fish, set forth among these choice fruits in a bowl, though members of a dull and stagnant-blooded race, appeared to know that there was something going on; and, to a fish, went gasping round and round their little world in slow and passionless excitement.

The Grocers'! oh, the Grocers'! nearly closed, with perhaps two shutters down, or one; but through those gaps such glimpses! It was not alone that the scales descending on the counter made a merry sound, or that the twine and roller parted company so briskly, or that the canisters were rattled up and down like juggling tricks, or even that the blended scents of tea and coffee were so grateful to the nose, or even that the raisins were so plentiful and rare, the almonds so extremely white, the sticks of cinnamon so long and straight, the other spices so delicious, the candied fruits so caked and spotted with molten sugar as to make the coldest lookers-on feel faint and subsequently bilious.

Nor was it that the figs were moist and pulpy, or that the French plums blushed in modest tartness from their highly-decorated boxes, or that everything was good to eat and in its Christmas dress; but the customers were all so hurried and so eager in the hopeful promise of the day, that they tumbled up against each other at the door, clashing their wicker baskets wildly, and left their purchases upon the counter, and came running back to fetch them, and committed hundreds of the like mistakes in the best humour possible; while the grocer and his people were so frank and fresh that the polished hearts with which they fastened their aprons behind might have been their own, worn outside for general inspection, and for Christmas daws to peck at if they chose.

But soon the steeples called good people all, to church and chapel, and away they came, flocking through the streets in their best clothes, and with their gayest faces. And at the same time there emerged from scores of by-streets, lanes, and nameless turnings, innumerable people, carrying their dinners to the bakers' shops[1].

The sight of these poor revellers appeared to interest the Spirit very much, for he stood with Scrooge beside him in a baker's doorway, and taking

---

1　當時的法令規定，在星期日和聖誕節，麵包店不能營業，所以窮人家要自己拿食材去麵包店烘焙，才有熟食可以吃。

2　在《聖經》裡，東方三賢士帶來三項禮物，其中一項就是乳香。

off the covers as their bearers passed, sprinkled incense[2] on their dinners from his torch.

And it was a very uncommon kind of torch, for once or twice when there were angry words between some dinner-carriers who had jostled each other, he shed a few drops of water on them from it, and their good humour was restored directly. For they said, it was a shame to quarrel upon Christmas Day. And so it was! God love it, so it was!

In time the bells ceased, and the bakers were shut up; and yet there was a genial shadowing forth of all these dinners and the progress of their cooking, in the thawed blotch of wet above each baker's oven; where the pavement smoked as if its stones were cooking too.

"Is there a peculiar flavour in what you sprinkle from your torch?" asked Scrooge.

"There is. My own."

"Would it apply to any kind of dinner on this day?" asked Scrooge.

"To any kindly given. To a poor one most."

"Why to a poor one most?" asked Scrooge.

"Because it needs it most."

"Spirit," said Scrooge, after a moment's thought, "I wonder you, of all the beings in the many worlds about us, should desire to cramp these people's opportunities of innocent enjoyment."

"I!" cried the Spirit.

"You would deprive them of their means of dining every seventh day, often the only day on which they can be said to dine at all," said Scrooge. "Wouldn't you?"

"I!" cried the Spirit.

"You seek to close these places on the Seventh Day?" said Scrooge. "And it comes to the same thing."

"I seek!" exclaimed the Spirit.

"Forgive me if I am wrong. It has been done in your name, or at least in that of your family[3]," said Scrooge.

"There are some upon this earth of yours," returned the Spirit, "who lay claim to know us, and who do their deeds of passion, pride, ill-will, hatred, envy, bigotry, and selfishness in our name, who are as strange to us and all our kith and kin, as if they had never lived. Remember that, and charge their doings on themselves, not us."

3　星期日是基督教的安息日，所以規定麵包店不能營業。又因為這位幽靈是「今日聖誕幽靈」，所以史古基假設幽靈是上帝派來的。

Scrooge promised that he would; and they went on, invisible, as they had been before, into the suburbs of the town. It was a remarkable quality of the Ghost (which Scrooge had observed at the baker's) that notwithstanding his gigantic size, he could accommodate himself to any place with ease; and that he stood beneath a low roof quite as gracefully and like a supernatural creature, as it was possible he could have done in any lofty hall.

And perhaps it was the pleasure the good Spirit had in showing off this power of his, or else it was his own kind, generous, hearty nature, and his sympathy with all poor men, that led him straight to Scrooge's clerk's; for there he went, and took Scrooge with him, holding to his robe; and on the threshold of the door the Spirit smiled, and stopped to bless Bob Cratchit's dwelling with the sprinkling of his torch. Think of that! Bob had but fifteen "Bob[4]" a-week himself; he pocketed on Saturdays but fifteen copies of his Christian name; and yet the Ghost of Christmas Present blessed his four-roomed house!

---

4 英文作「Bob」，Bob是人名「鮑伯」，也是英俚語「先令」的意思。

Then up rose Mrs. Cratchit, Cratchit's wife, dressed out but poorly in a twice-turned gown, but brave in ribbons, which are cheap, and make a goodly show for sixpence; and she laid the cloth, assisted by Belinda Cratchit, second of her daughters, also brave in ribbons; while Master Peter Cratchit plunged a fork into the saucepan of potatoes, and getting the corners of his monstrous shirt-collar (Bob's private property, conferred upon his son and heir in honour of the day) into his mouth, rejoiced to find himself so gallantly attired, and yearned to show his linen in the fashionable Parks.

And now two smaller Cratchits, boy and girl, came tearing in, screaming that outside the baker's they had smelt the goose, and known it for their own; and basking in luxurious thoughts of sage and onion, these young Cratchits danced about the table, and exalted Master Peter Cratchit to the skies, while he (not proud, although his

Tiny Tim

collars nearly choked him) blew the fire, until the slow potatoes bubbling up, knocked loudly at the saucepan-lid to be let out and peeled.

"What has ever got your precious father, then," said Mrs. Cratchit. "And your brother, Tiny Tim; and Martha warn't as late last Christmas Day by half-an-hour?"

"Here's Martha, mother!" said a girl, appearing as she spoke.

"Here's Martha, mother!" cried the two young Cratchits. "Hurrah! There's *such* a goose, Martha!"

"Why, bless your heart alive, my dear, how late you are!" said Mrs. Cratchit, kissing her a dozen times, and taking off her shawl and bonnet for her, with officious zeal.

"We'd a deal of work to finish up last night," replied the girl, "and had to clear away this morning, mother!"

"Well! Never mind so long as you are come," said Mrs. Cratchit. "Sit ye down before the fire, my dear, and have a warm, Lord bless ye!"

"No, no! There's father coming," cried the two young Cratchits, who were everywhere at once. "Hide, Martha, hide!"

He had been Tim's blood horse
all the way from church.

So Martha hid herself, and in came little Bob, the father, with at least three feet of comforter exclusive of the fringe, hanging down before him; and his thread-bare clothes darned up and brushed, to look seasonable, and Tiny Tim upon his shoulder. Alas for Tiny Tim, he bore a little crutch, and had his limbs supported by an iron frame!

"Why, where's our Martha?" cried Bob Cratchit, looking round.

"Not coming," said Mrs. Cratchit.

"Not coming!" said Bob, with a sudden declension in his high spirits; for he had been Tim's blood horse all the way from church, and had come home rampant. "Not coming upon Christmas day!"

Martha didn't like to see him disappointed, if it were only in joke; so she came out prematurely from behind the closet door, and ran into his arms, while the two young Cratchits hustled Tiny Tim, and bore him off into the wash-house, that he might hear the pudding singing in the copper.

"And how did little Tim behave?" asked Mrs. Cratchit, when she had rallied Bob on his credulity and Bob had hugged his daughter to his heart's content.

"As good as gold," said Bob, "and better. Somehow he gets thoughtful sitting by himself so much, and thinks the strangest things you ever heard. He told me, coming home, that he hoped the people saw him in the church, because he was a cripple, and it might be pleasant to them to remember upon Christmas Day, who made lame beggars walk and blind men see."

Bob's voice was tremulous when he told them this, and trembled more when he said that Tiny Tim was growing strong and hearty.

His active little crutch was heard upon the floor, and back came Tiny Tim before another word was spoken, escorted by his brother and sister to his stool before the fire; and while Bob, turning up his cuffs—as if, poor fellow, they were capable of being made more shabby— compounded some hot mixture in a jug with gin and lemons, and stirred it round and round and put it on the hob to simmer; Master Peter and the two ubiquitous young Cratchits went to fetch the goose, with which they soon returned in high procession.

Such a bustle ensued that you might have thought a goose the rarest of all birds; a feathered phenomenon, to which a black swan was a matter of course; and in truth it was something very like it in that house.

Mrs. Cratchit made the gravy (ready beforehand in a little saucepan) hissing hot; Master Peter mashed the potatoes with incredible vigour; Miss Belinda sweetened up the apple-sauce; Martha dusted the hot plates; Bob took Tiny Tim beside him in a tiny corner at the table; the two young Cratchits set chairs for everybody, not forgetting

Tiny Tim

themselves, and mounting guard upon their posts, crammed spoons into their mouths, lest they should shriek for goose before their turn came to be helped.

At last the dishes were set on, and grace was said. It was succeeded by a breathless pause, as Mrs. Cratchit, looking slowly all along the carving-knife, prepared to plunge it in the breast; but when she did, and when the long expected gush of stuffing issued forth, one murmur of delight arose all round the board, and even Tiny Tim, excited by the two young Cratchits, beat on the table with the handle of his knife, and feebly cried "Hurrah!"

There never was such a goose. Bob said he didn't believe there ever was such a goose cooked. Its tenderness and flavour, size and cheapness, were the themes of universal admiration. Eked out by the apple-sauce and mashed potatoes, it was a sufficient dinner for the whole family; indeed, as Mrs. Cratchit said with great delight (surveying one small atom of a bone upon the dish), they hadn't ate it all at last! Yet every one had had enough, and the youngest Cratchits in particular, were steeped in sage and onion to the eyebrows! But now, the plates being changed by Miss Belinda, Mrs. Cratchit left the room alone—too nervous to bear witnesses—to take the pudding up, and bring it in.

Suppose it should not be done enough! Suppose it should break in turning out! Suppose somebody should have got over the wall of the back-yard, and stolen it, while they were merry with the goose—a supposition at which the two young Cratchits became livid! All sorts of horrors were supposed.

Hallo! A great deal of steam! The pudding was out of the copper[5]. A smell like a washing-day! That was the

---

5　煮布丁的銅鍋，平時是洗衣服用的。

Mrs. Cratchit entered: flushed, but smiling proudly, with the pudding.

cloth. A smell like an eating-house and a pastry cook's next door to each other, with a laundress's next door to that! That was the pudding! In half a minute Mrs. Cratchit entered—flushed, but smiling proudly, with the pudding, like a speckled cannon-ball, so hard and firm, blazing in half of half-a-quartern of ignited brandy, and bedight with Christmas holly stuck into the top.

Oh, a wonderful pudding! Bob Cratchit said, and calmly too, that he regarded it as the greatest success achieved by Mrs. Cratchit since their marriage. Mrs. Cratchit said that now the weight was off her mind, she would confess she had had her doubts about the quantity of flour. Everybody had something to say about it, but nobody said or thought it was at all a small pudding for a large family. It would have been flat heresy to do so. Any Cratchit would have blushed to hint at such a thing.

At last the dinner was all done, the cloth was cleared, the hearth swept, and the fire made up. The compound in the jug being tasted, and considered perfect, apples and oranges were put upon the table, and a shovelful of chestnuts on the fire. Then all the Cratchit family drew round the hearth, in what Bob Cratchit called a circle, meaning half a one; and at Bob

Then all the Cratchit family drew round the hearth.

Cratchit's elbow stood the family display of glass; two tumblers, and a custard-cup without a handle.

These held the hot stuff from the jug, however, as well as golden goblets would have done; and Bob served it out with beaming looks, while the chestnuts on the fire sputtered and crackled noisily. Then Bob proposed:

"A merry Christmas to us all, my dears. God bless us!"

Which all the family re-echoed.

"God bless us every one!" said Tiny Tim, the last of all.

He sat very close to his father's side, upon his little stool. Bob held his withered little hand in his, as if he loved the child, and wished to keep him by his side, and dreaded that he might be taken from him.

"Spirit," said Scrooge, with an interest he had never felt before, "tell me if Tiny Tim will live."

"I see a vacant seat," replied the Ghost, "in the poor chimney corner, and a crutch without an owner, carefully preserved. If these shadows remain unaltered by the Future, the child will die."

"No, no," said Scrooge. "Oh no, kind Spirit! say he will be spared."

"God bless us every one!" said Tiny Tim.

"If these shadows remain unaltered by the Future, none other of my race," returned the Ghost, "will find him here. What then? If he be like to die, he had better do it, and decrease the surplus population."

Scrooge hung his head to hear his own words quoted by the Spirit, and was overcome with penitence and grief.

"Man," said the Ghost, "if man you be in heart, not adamant, forbear that wicked cant until you have discovered what the surplus is, and where it is. Will you decide what men shall live, what men shall die? It may be, that in the sight of Heaven, you are more worthless and less fit to live than millions like this poor man's child. Oh God! to hear the insect on the leaf pronouncing on the too much life among his hungry brothers in the dust!"

Scrooge bent before the Ghost's rebuke, and trembling cast his eyes upon the ground. But he raised them speedily, on hearing his own name.

"Mr. Scrooge!" said Bob; "I'll give you Mr. Scrooge, the Founder of the Feast!"

"The Founder of the Feast indeed!" cried Mrs. Cratchit, reddening. "I wish I had him here. I'd give him a piece of my mind to feast upon, and I hope he'd

"Mr. Scrooge!" said Bob; "I'll give you Mr. Scrooge, the Founder of the Feast!"

have a good appetite for it."

"My dear," said Bob, "the children; Christmas Day."

"It should be Christmas Day, I am sure," said she, "on which one drinks the health of such an odious, stingy, hard, unfeeling man as Mr. Scrooge. You know he is, Robert! Nobody knows it better than you do, poor fellow!"

"My dear," was Bob's mild answer, "Christmas Day."

"I'll drink his health for your sake and the Day's," said Mrs. Cratchit, "not for his. Long life to him! A merry Christmas and a happy New Year! He'll be very merry and very happy, I have no doubt!"

The children drank the toast after her. It was the first of their proceedings which had no heartiness in it. Tiny Tim drank it last of all, but he didn't care twopence for it. Scrooge was the Ogre of the family. The mention of his name cast a dark shadow on the party, which was not dispelled for full five minutes.

After it had passed away, they were ten times merrier than before, from the mere relief of Scrooge the Baleful being done with. Bob Cratchit told them how he had a situation in his eye for Master Peter, which would bring in, if obtained, full five-and-sixpence weekly. The two young Cratchits laughed tremendously at the idea of Peter's being a man of business; and Peter himself looked thoughtfully at the fire from between his collars, as if he were deliberating what particular investments he should favour when he came into the receipt of that bewildering income.

Martha, who was a poor apprentice at a milliner's, then told them what kind of work she had to do, and how many hours she worked at a stretch, and how she meant to lie abed tomorrow morning for a good long rest; tomorrow being a holiday she passed at home. Also how she had seen a countess and a lord some days before, and how the lord "was much about as tall as Peter;" at which Peter pulled up his collars so high that you couldn't have seen his head if you had been there. All this time the chestnuts and the jug went round and round; and bye and bye they had a song, about a lost child travelling in the snow, from Tiny Tim; who had a plaintive little voice, and sang it very well indeed.

There was nothing of high mark in this. They were not a handsome family; they were not well dressed; their shoes were far from being waterproof; their clothes were scanty; and Peter might have known, and very likely did, the inside of a pawnbroker's. But they were happy, grateful, pleased with one another, and contented with the time; and when they faded, and looked happier yet in the bright sprinklings of the Spirit's torch at parting, Scrooge had his eye upon them, and especially on Tiny Tim, until the last.

By this time it was getting dark, and snowing pretty heavily; and as Scrooge and the Spirit went along the streets, the brightness of the roaring fires in kitchens, parlours, and all sorts of rooms, was wonderful. Here, the flickering of the blaze showed preparations for a cosy dinner, with hot plates baking through and through before the fire, and deep red curtains, ready to be drawn, to shut out cold and darkness. There, all the children of the house were running out into the snow to meet their married sisters, brothers, cousins, uncles, aunts, and be the first to greet them. Here, again, were shadows on the window-blind of guests assembling; and there a group of handsome girls, all hooded and fur-booted, and all chattering at once, tripped lightly off to some near neighbour's house; where, woe upon the single man who saw them enter—artful witches: well they knew it—in a glow!

But if you had judged from the numbers of people on their way to friendly gatherings, you might have thought that no one was at home to give them welcome when they got there, instead of every house expecting company, and piling up its fires half-chimney high. Blessings on it, how the Ghost exulted! How it bared its breadth of breast, and opened its capacious palm, and floated on, outpouring, with a generous hand, its bright and harmless mirth on everything within its reach! The very lamplighter, who ran on before, dotting the dusky street with specks of light, and who was dressed to spend the evening somewhere, laughed out loudly as the Spirit passed: though little kenned the lamplighter that he had any company but Christmas.

And now, without a word of warning from the Ghost, they stood upon a bleak and desert moor, where monstrous masses of rude stone were cast about, as though it were the burial-place of giants; and water spread itself wheresoever it listed—or would have done so, but for the frost that held it prisoner; and nothing grew but moss and furze, and coarse, rank grass. Down in the west the setting sun had left a streak of fiery red, which glared upon the desolation for an instant, like a sullen eye, and frowning lower, lower, lower yet, was lost in the thick gloom of darkest night.

"What place is this?" asked Scrooge.

"A place where miners live, who labour in the bowels of the earth," returned the Spirit. "But they know me. See!"

A light shone from the window of a hut, and swiftly they advanced towards it. Passing through the wall of mud and stone, they found a cheerful company assembled round a glowing fire. An old, old man and woman, with their children and their children's children, and another generation beyond that, all decked out gaily in their holiday attire. The old man, in a voice that seldom rose above the howling of the wind upon the barren waste, was singing them a Christmas song; it had been a very old song when he was a boy; and from time to time they all joined in the chorus. So surely as they raised their voices, the old man got quite blithe and loud; and so surely as they stopped, his vigour sang again.

The Spirit did not tarry here, but bade Scrooge hold his robe, and passing on above the moor, sped whither? Not to sea? To sea. To Scrooge's horror, looking back, he saw the last of the land, a frightful range of rocks, behind them; and his ears were deafened by the thundering of water, as it rolled, and roared, and raged among the dreadful caverns it had worn, and fiercely tried to undermine the earth.

Built upon a dismal reef of sunken rocks, some league or so from shore, on which the waters chafed and dashed, the wild year through, there stood a solitary lighthouse. Great heaps of sea-weed clung to its base, and storm-birds—born of the wind one might suppose, as sea-weed of the water—rose and fell about it, like the waves they skimmed.

But even here, two men who watched the light had made a fire, that through the loophole in the thick stone wall shed out a ray of brightness on the awful sea. Joining their horny hands over the rough table at which they sat, they wished each other merry Christmas in their can of grog; and one of them: the elder, too, with his face all damaged and scarred with hard weather, as the figure-head of an old ship might be: struck up a sturdy song that was like a gale in itself.

Again the Ghost sped on, above the black and heaving sea—on, on—until, being far away, as he told Scrooge, from any shore, they lighted on a ship. They stood beside the helmsman at the wheel, the look-out in the bow, the officers who had the watch; dark, ghostly figures in their several stations; but every man among them hummed a Christmas tune, or had a Christmas thought, or spoke below his breath to his companion of some bygone Christmas Day, with homeward hopes belonging to it. And every man on board, waking or sleeping, good or bad, had had a kinder word for another on that day than on any day in the year; and had shared to some extent in its festivities; and had remembered those he cared for at a distance, and had known that they delighted to remember him.

It was a great surprise to Scrooge, while listening to the moaning of the wind, and thinking what a solemn thing it was to move on through the lonely darkness over an unknown abyss, whose depths were secrets as profound as death: it was a great surprise to Scrooge, while thus engaged, to hear a hearty laugh. It was a much greater surprise to Scrooge to recognise it as his own nephew's, and to find himself in a bright, dry, gleaming room, with the Spirit standing smiling by his side, and looking at that same nephew with approving affability!

"Ha, ha!" laughed Scrooge's nephew. "Ha, ha, ha!"

If you should happen, by any unlikely chance, to know a man more blessed in a laugh than Scrooge's nephew, all I can say is, I should like to know him too. Introduce him to me, and I'll cultivate his acquaintance.

It is a fair, even-handed, noble adjustment of things, that while there is infection in disease and sorrow, there is nothing in the world so irresistibly contagious as laughter and good-humour. When Scrooge's nephew laughed in this way—holding his sides, rolling his head, and twisting his face into the most extravagant contortions—Scrooge's niece, by marriage, laughed as heartily as he. And their assembled friends being not a bit behindhand, roared out lustily.

"Ha, ha! Ha, ha, ha, ha!"

"He said that Christmas was a humbug, as I live!" cried Scrooge's nephew. "He believed it too!"

"More shame for him, Fred!" said Scrooge's niece, indignantly. Bless those women; they never do anything by halves. They are always in earnest.

She was very pretty; exceedingly pretty. With a dimpled, surprised-looking, capital face; a ripe little mouth, that seemed made to be kissed—as no doubt it was; all kinds of good little dots about her chin, that melted into one another when she laughed; and the sunniest pair of eyes you ever saw in any little creature's head. Altogether she was what you would have called provoking, you know; but satisfactory, too. Oh, perfectly satisfactory!

"He's a comical old fellow," said Scrooge's nephew, "that's the truth; and not so pleasant as he might be. However, his offences carry their own punishment, and I have nothing to say against him."

"I'm sure he is very rich, Fred," hinted Scrooge's niece. "At least you always tell *me* so."

"What of that, my dear!" said Scrooge's nephew. "His wealth is of no use to him. He don't do any good with it. He don't make himself comfortable with it. He hasn't the satisfaction of thinking—ha, ha, ha!—that he is ever going to benefit Us with it."

"I have no patience with him," observed Scrooge's niece. Scrooge's niece's sisters, and all the other ladies, expressed the same opinion.

"Oh, I have!" said Scrooge's nephew. "I am sorry for him; I couldn't be angry with him if I tried. Who suffers by his ill whims! Himself, always. Here, he takes it into his head to dislike us, and he won't come and dine with us. What's the consequence? He don't lose much of a dinner."

"Indeed, I think he loses a very good dinner," interrupted Scrooge's niece. Everybody else said the same, and they must be allowed to have been competent judges, because they had just had dinner;

and with the dessert upon the table, were clustered round the fire, by lamplight.

"Well! I'm very glad to hear it," said Scrooge's nephew, "because I haven't great faith in these young housekeepers. What do *you* say, Topper?"

Topper had clearly got his eye upon one of Scrooge's niece's sisters, for he answered that a bachelor was a wretched outcast, who had no right to express an opinion on the subject. Whereat Scrooge's niece's sister—the plump one with the lace tucker: not the one with the roses—blushed.

"Do go on, Fred," said Scrooge's niece, clapping her hands. "He never finishes what he begins to say! He is such a ridiculous fellow!"

Scrooge's nephew revelled in another laugh, and as it was impossible to keep the infection off; though the plump sister tried hard to do it with aromatic vinegar[6], his example was unanimously followed.

"I was only going to say," said Scrooge's nephew, "that the consequence of his taking a dislike to us, and not making merry with us, is, as I think, that he loses some pleasant moments, which could do him no

6　芳香療法，用來預防頭痛。

harm. I am sure he loses pleasanter companions than he can find in his own thoughts, either in his mouldy old office or his dusty chambers. I mean to give him the same chance every year, whether he likes it or not, for I pity him. He may rail at Christmas till he dies, but he can't help thinking better of it—I defy him—if he finds me going there, in good temper, year after year, and saying Uncle Scrooge, how are you? If it only puts him in the vein to leave his poor clerk fifty pounds, *that's* something; and I think I shook him, yesterday."

It was their turn to laugh now, at the notion of his shaking Scrooge. But being thoroughly good-natured, and not much caring what they laughed at, so that they laughed at any rate, he encouraged them in their merriment, and passed the bottle, joyously.

After tea, they had some music. For they were a musical family, and knew what they were about, when they sung a Glee or Catch, I can assure you: especially Topper, who could growl away in the bass like a good one, and never swell the large veins in his forehead, or get red in the face over it.

Scrooge's niece played well upon the harp; and played among other tunes a simple little air (a mere nothing: you might learn to whistle it in two minutes), which had been familiar to the child who fetched Scrooge from the boarding-school, as he had been reminded by the Ghost of Christmas Past.

When this strain of music sounded, all the things that Ghost had shown him, came upon his mind; he softened more and more; and thought that if he could have listened to it often, years ago, he might have cultivated the kindnesses of life for his own happiness with his own hands, without resorting to the sexton's spade that buried Jacob Marley.

But they didn't devote the whole evening to music. After a while they played at forfeits; for it is good to be children sometimes, and never better than at Christmas, when its mighty Founder was a child himself.

Stop! There was first a game at blind-man's buff. Of course there was. And I no more believe Topper was really blind than I believe he had eyes in his boots. My opinion is, that it was a done thing between him and Scrooge's nephew; and that the Ghost of Christmas Present knew it. The way he went after that plump sister in the lace tucker, was an outrage on the credulity of human nature. Knocking down the fire-irons, tumbling over the chairs, bumping against the piano, smothering himself among the curtains, wherever she

The way he went after that plump sister in the lace tucker.

went, there went he. He always knew where the plump sister was. He wouldn't catch anybody else. If you had fallen up against him, (as some of them did), on purpose, he would have made a feint of endeavouring to seize you, which would have been an affront to your understanding; and would instantly have sidled off in the direction of the plump sister.

She often cried out that it wasn't fair; and it really was not. But when at last, he caught her; when, in spite of all her silken rustlings, and her rapid flutterings past him, he got her into a corner whence there was no escape; then his conduct was the most execrable. For his pretending not to know her; his pretending that it was necessary to touch her head-dress, and further to assure himself of her identity by pressing a certain ring upon her finger, and a certain chain about her neck; was vile, monstrous! No doubt she told him her opinion of it, when, another blind-man being in office, they were so very confidential together, behind the curtains.

Scrooge's niece was not one of the blind-man's buff party, but was made comfortable with a large chair and a footstool, in a snug corner, where the Ghost and Scrooge were close behind her. But she joined in the forfeits, and loved her love to admiration with all the letters of the alphabet. Likewise at the game of How, When, and Where, she was very great, and to the secret joy of Scrooge's nephew, beat her sisters hollow: though they were sharp girls too, as Topper could have told you.

There might have been twenty people there, young and old, but they all played, and so did Scrooge; for wholly forgetting in the interest he had in what was going on, that his voice made no sound in their ears, he sometimes came out with his guess quite loud, and very often guessed quite right, too; for the sharpest needle, best Whitechapel, warranted not to cut in the eye, was not sharper than Scrooge, blunt as he took it in his head to be.

The Ghost was greatly pleased to find him in this mood, and looked upon him with such favour that he begged like a boy to be allowed to stay until the guests departed. But this the Spirit said could not be done.

"Here's a new game," said Scrooge. "One half hour, Spirit, only one!"

It was a game called Yes and No, where Scrooge's nephew had to think of something, and the rest must find out what; he only answering to their questions yes or no as the case was. The brisk fire of questioning to which he was exposed, elicited from him that he was thinking of an animal, a live animal, rather a disagreeable animal, a savage animal, an animal that growled and grunted sometimes, and talked sometimes, and lived in London, and walked about the streets, and wasn't made a show of, and wasn't led by anybody, and didn't live in a menagerie, and was never killed in a market, and was not a horse, or an ass, or a cow, or a bull, or a tiger, or a dog, or a pig, or a cat, or a bear.

At every fresh question that was put to him, this nephew burst into a fresh roar of laughter; and was so inexpressibly tickled, that he was obliged to get up off the sofa and stamp. At last the plump sister, falling into a similar state, cried out:

"I have found it out! I know what it is, Fred! I know what it is!"

"What is it?" cried Fred.

"It's your uncle Scro-o-o-o-oge!"

Which it certainly was. Admiration was the universal sentiment, though some objected that the reply to "Is it a bear[7]?" ought to have been "Yes;" inasmuch as an

---

7 bear 也可指粗魯、不禮貌的人。

At every fresh question that was put to him,
this nephew burst into a fresh roar of laughter.

answer in the negative was sufficient to have diverted their thoughts from Mr. Scrooge, supposing they had ever had any tendency that way.

"He has given us plenty of merriment, I am sure," said Fred, "and it would be ungrateful not to drink his health. Here is a glass of mulled wine ready to our hand at the moment; and I say 'Uncle Scrooge!' "

"Well! Uncle Scrooge!" they cried.

"A merry Christmas and a happy New Year to the old man, whatever he is!" said Scrooge's nephew. "He wouldn't take it from me, but may he have it, nevertheless. Uncle Scrooge!"

Uncle Scrooge had imperceptibly become so gay and light of heart, that he would have pledged the unconscious company in return, and thanked them in an inaudible speech, if the Ghost had given him time. But the whole scene passed off in the breath of the last word spoken by his nephew; and he and the Spirit were again upon their travels.

Much they saw, and far they went, and many homes they visited, but always with a happy end. The Spirit stood beside sick beds, and they were cheerful; on foreign lands, and they were close at home; by struggling men, and they were patient in their greater hope; by poverty, and it was rich. In almshouse, hospital, and jail, in misery's every refuge, where vain man in his little brief authority had not made fast the door, and barred the Spirit out, he left his blessing, and taught Scrooge his precepts.

It was a long night, if it were only a night; but Scrooge had his doubts of this, because the Christmas holidays appeared to be condensed into the space of time they passed together. It was strange, too, that while Scrooge remained unaltered in his outward form, the Ghost grew older, clearly older. Scrooge had observed this change, but never spoke of it, until they left a children's Twelfth Night party, when, looking at the Spirit as they stood together in an open place, he noticed that its hair was gray.

"Are Spirits' lives so short?" asked Scrooge.

"My life upon this globe, is very brief," replied the Ghost. "It ends tonight."

"Tonight!" cried Scrooge.

"Tonight at midnight. Hark! The time is drawing near."

The chimes were ringing the three quarters past eleven at that moment.

"Forgive me if I am not justified in what I ask," said

Scrooge, looking intently at the Spirit's robe, "but I see something strange, and not belonging to yourself, protruding from your skirts. Is it a foot or a claw?"

"It might be a claw, for the flesh there is upon it," was the Spirit's sorrowful reply. "Look here."

From the foldings of its robe, it brought two children, wretched, abject, frightful, hideous, miserable. They knelt down at its feet, and clung upon the outside of its garment.

"Oh Man! look here. Look, look down here!" exclaimed the Ghost.

They were a boy and girl. Yellow, meagre, ragged, scowling, wolfish, but prostrate, too, in their humility. Where graceful youth should have filled their features out, and touched them with its freshest tints, a stale and shrivelled hand, like that of age, had pinched, and twisted them, and pulled them into shreds. Where angels might have sat enthroned, devils lurked, and glared out menacing. No change, no degradation, no perversion of humanity, in any grade, through all the mysteries of wonderful creation, has monsters half so horrible and dread.

Scrooge started back, appalled. Having them shown to him in this way, he tried to say they were fine children, but the words choked themselves, rather than be parties to a lie of such enormous magnitude.

"Spirit! are they yours?" Scrooge could say no more.

"They are Man's," said the Spirit, looking down upon them. "And they cling to me, appealing from their fathers. This boy is Ignorance. This girl is Want. Beware them both, and all of their degree, but most of all beware this boy, for on his brow I see that written which is Doom, unless the writing be erased. Deny it!" cried the Spirit, stretching out its hand towards the city. "Slander those who tell it ye! Admit it for your factious purposes, and make it worse! And bide the end!"

"Have they no refuge or resource?" cried Scrooge.

"Are there no prisons?" said the Spirit, turning on him for the last time with his own words. "Are there no workhouses?"

The bell struck twelve.

Scrooge looked about him for the Ghost, and saw it not. As the last stroke ceased to vibrate, he remembered the prediction of old Jacob Marley, and lifting up his eyes, beheld a solemn Phantom, draped and hooded, coming, like a mist along the ground, towards him.

Stave Four

The Last of the Spirits

The Phantom slowly, gravely, silently, approached. When it came near him, Scrooge bent down upon his knee; for in the very air through which this Spirit moved it seemed to scatter gloom and mystery.

It was shrouded in a deep black garment, which concealed its head, its face, its form, and left nothing of it visible save one outstretched hand. But for this it would have been difficult to detach its figure from the night, and separate it from the darkness by which it was surrounded.

He felt that it was tall and stately when it came beside him, and that its mysterious presence filled him with a solemn dread. He knew no more, for the Spirit neither spoke nor moved.

"I am in the presence of the Ghost of Christmas Yet To Come?" said Scrooge.

The Spirit answered not,
but pointed onward with its hand.

The Spirit answered not, but pointed onward with its hand.

"You are about to show me shadows of the things that have not happened, but will happen in the time before us," Scrooge pursued. "Is that so, Spirit?"

The upper portion of the garment was contracted for an instant in its folds, as if the Spirit had inclined its head. That was the only answer he received.

Although well used to ghostly company by this time, Scrooge feared the silent shape so much that his legs trembled beneath him, and he found that he could hardly stand when he prepared to follow it. The Spirit paused a moment, as observing his condition, and giving him time to recover.

But Scrooge was all the worse for this. It thrilled him with a vague uncertain horror, to know that behind the dusky shroud, there were ghostly eyes intently fixed upon him, while he, though he stretched his own to the utmost, could see nothing but a spectral hand and one great heap of black.

"Ghost of the Future!" he exclaimed, "I fear you more than any Spectre I have seen. But as I know your purpose is to do me good, and as I hope to live to be another man from what I was, I am prepared to bear you company, and do it with a thankful heart. Will you not speak to me?"

It gave him no reply. The hand was pointed straight before them.

"Lead on!" said Scrooge. "Lead on! The night is waning fast, and it is precious time to me, I know. Lead on, Spirit!"

The Phantom moved away as it had come towards him. Scrooge followed in the shadow of its dress, which bore him up, he thought, and carried him along.

They scarcely seemed to enter the city; for the city rather seemed to spring up about them, and encompass them of its own act. But there they were, in the heart of it; on 'Change, amongst the merchants; who hurried up and down, and chinked the money in their pockets, and conversed in groups, and looked at their watches, and trifled thoughtfully with their great gold seals; and so forth, as Scrooge had seen them often.

The Spirit stopped beside one little knot of business men. Observing that the hand was pointed to them, Scrooge advanced to listen to their talk.

"No," said a great fat man with a monstrous chin, "I don't know much about it either way. I only know he's

I only know he's dead.

dead."

"When did he die?" inquired another.

"Last night, I believe."

"Why, what was the matter with him?" asked a third, taking a vast quantity of snuff out of a very large snuff-box. "I thought he'd never die."

"God knows," said the first, with a yawn.

"What has he done with his money?" asked a red-faced gentleman with a pendulous excrescence on the end of his nose, that shook like the gills of a turkey-cock.

"I haven't heard," said the man with the large chin, yawning again. "Left it to his Company, perhaps. He hasn't left it to *me*. That's all I know."

This pleasantry was received with a general laugh.

"It's likely to be a very cheap funeral," said the same speaker; "for upon my life I don't know of anybody to go to it. Suppose we make up a party and volunteer?"

"I don't mind going if a lunch is provided," observed the gentleman with the excrescence on his nose. "But I must be fed if I make one."

Another laugh.

"Well, I am the most disinterested among you, after all," said the first speaker, "for I never wear black

This pleasantry was received with a general laugh.

gloves, and I never eat lunch. But I'll offer to go if anybody else will. When I come to think of it, I'm not at all sure that I wasn't his most particular friend; for we used to stop and speak whenever we met. Bye, bye!"

Speakers and listeners strolled away, and mixed with other groups. Scrooge knew the men, and looked towards the Spirit for an explanation.

The Phantom glided on into a street. Its finger pointed to two persons meeting. Scrooge listened again, thinking that the explanation might lie here.

He knew these men, also, perfectly. They were men of business: very wealthy, and of great importance. He had made a point always of standing well in their esteem in a business point of view, that is; strictly in a business point of view.

"How are you?" said one.

"How are you?" returned the other.

"Well!" said the first. "Old Scratch has got his own at last, hey?"

"So I am told," returned the second. "Cold, isn't it?"

"Seasonable for Christmas time. You are not a skater, I suppose?"

"No. No. Something else to think of. Good morning!"

Not another word. That was their meeting, their

conversation, and their parting.

Scrooge was at first inclined to be surprised that the Spirit should attach importance to conversations apparently so trivial; but feeling assured that they must have some hidden purpose, he set himself to consider what it was likely to be. They could scarcely be supposed to have any bearing on the death of Jacob, his old partner, for that was Past, and this Ghost's province was the Future. Nor could he think of any one immediately connected with himself, to whom he could apply them. But nothing doubting that to whomsoever they applied they had some latent moral for his own improvement, he resolved to treasure up every word he heard, and everything he saw, and especially to observe the shadow of himself when it appeared. For he had an expectation that the conduct of his future self would give him the clue he missed, and would render the solution of these riddles easy.

He looked about in that very place for his own image; but another man stood in his accustomed corner, and though the clock pointed to his usual time of day for being there, he saw no likeness of himself among the multitudes that poured in through the Porch. It gave him little surprise, however; for he had been revolving in his mind a change of life, and thought and hoped he saw his new-born resolutions carried out in this.

Quiet and dark, beside him stood the Phantom, with its outstretched hand. When he roused himself from his thoughtful quest, he fancied from the turn of the hand, and its situation in reference to himself, that the Unseen Eyes were looking at him keenly. It made him shudder, and feel very cold.

They left the busy scene, and went into an obscure part of the town, where Scrooge had never penetrated before although he recognised its situation, and its bad repute. The ways were foul and narrow; the shops and houses wretched; the people half-naked, drunken, slipshod, ugly. Alleys and archways, like so many cesspools, disgorged their offences of smell, and dirt, and life, upon the straggling streets; and the whole quarter reeked with crime, with filth, and misery.

Far in this den of infamous resort, there was a low-browed, beetling shop, below a pent-house roof, where iron, old rags, bottles, bones, and greasy offal, were bought. Upon the floor within, were piled up heaps of rusty keys, nails, chains, hinges, files, scales, weights, and refuse iron of all kinds. Secrets that few would like to scrutinise were bred and hidden in mountains of unseemly rags, masses of corrupted fat, and sepulchres of bones.

Sitting in among the wares he dealt in, by a charcoal-stove, made of old bricks, was a grey-haired rascal, nearly seventy years of age; who had screened himself from the cold air without, by a frousy curtaining of miscellaneous tatters, hung upon a line; and smoked his pipe in all the luxury of calm retirement.

Scrooge and the Phantom came into the presence of this man, just as a woman with a heavy bundle slunk into the shop. But she had scarcely entered, when another woman, similarly laden, came in too; and she was closely followed by a man in faded black, who was no less startled by the sight of them, than they had been upon the recognition of each other. After a short period of blank astonishment, in which the old man with the pipe had joined them, they all three burst into a laugh.

"Let the charwoman alone to be the first!" cried she who had entered first. "Let the laundress alone to be the second; and let the undertaker's man alone to be the third. Look here, old Joe, here's a chance! If we haven't all three met here without meaning it!"

"You couldn't have met in a better place," said old Joe, removing his pipe from his mouth. "Come into the parlour. You were made free of it long ago, you know; and the other two an't strangers. Stop till I shut the door of the shop. Ah! How it skreeks! There an't such a rusty bit of metal in the place as its own hinges, I believe; and I'm sure there's no such old bones here, as mine. Ha, ha! We're all suitable to our calling, we're well matched. Come into the parlour. Come into the parlour."

The parlour was the space behind the screen of rags. The old man raked the fire together with an old stair-rod, and having trimmed his smoky lamp (for it was night), with the stem of his pipe, put it in his mouth again.

While he did this, the woman who had already spoken threw her bundle on the floor and sat down in a flaunting manner on a stool; crossing her elbows on her knees, and looking with a bold defiance at the other two.

"What odds then? What odds, Mrs. Dilber?" said the woman. "Every person has a right to take care of themselves. *He* always did."

"That's true, indeed!" said the laundress. "No man more so."

"Why then, don't stand staring as if you was afraid, woman! Who's the wiser? We're not going to pick holes in each other's coats, I suppose?"

"No, indeed!" said Mrs. Dilber and the man together. "We should hope not."

"Very well, then!" cried the woman. "That's enough. Who's the worse for the loss of a few things like these? Not a dead man, I suppose."

"No, indeed," said Mrs. Dilber, laughing.

"If he wanted to keep 'em after he was dead, a wicked old screw," pursued the woman, "why wasn't he natural in his lifetime? If he had been, he'd have had somebody to look after him when he was struck with Death, instead of lying gasping out his last there, alone by himself."

"It's the truest word that ever was spoke," said Mrs. Dilber. "It's a judgment on him."

"I wish it was a little heavier one," replied the woman; "and it should have been, you may depend upon it, if I could have laid my hands on anything else. Open that bundle, old Joe, and let me know the value of it. Speak out plain. I'm not afraid to be the first, nor afraid for them to see it. We knew pretty well that we were helping ourselves before we met here, I believe. It's no sin. Open the bundle, Joe."

But the gallantry of her friends would not allow of this; and the man in faded black, mounting the breach first, produced *his* plunder. It was not extensive. A seal or two, a pencil-case, a pair of sleeve-buttons, and a brooch of no great value, were all. They were severally examined and appraised by old Joe, who chalked the sums he was disposed to give for each, upon the wall, and added them up into a total when he found there was nothing more to come.

"That's your account," said Joe, "and I wouldn't give another sixpence, if I was to be boiled for not doing it. Who's next?"

Mrs. Dilber was next. Sheets and towels, a little wearing apparel, two old-fashioned silver teaspoons, a pair of sugar-tongs, and a few boots. Her account was stated on the wall in the same manner.

"I always give too much to ladies. It's a weakness of mine, and that's the way I ruin myself," said old Joe. "That's your account. If you asked me for another penny, and made it an open question, I'd repent of being so liberal and knock off half-a-crown."

"And now undo *my* bundle, Joe," said the first woman.

Joe went down on his knees for the greater convenience of opening it, and having unfastened a great many knots, dragged out a large and heavy roll of some dark stuff.

"What do you call this?" said Joe. "Bed-curtains!"

"Ah!" returned the woman, laughing and leaning forward on her crossed arms. "Bed-curtains!"

"You don't mean to say you took 'em down, rings and all, with him lying there?" said Joe.

"Yes, I do," replied the woman. "Why not?"

"You were born to make your fortune," said Joe, "and you'll certainly do it."

"I certainly shan't hold my hand, when I can get anything in it by reaching it out, for the sake of such a man as He was, I promise you, Joe," returned the woman coolly. "Don't drop that oil upon the blankets, now."

"His blankets?" asked Joe.

"Whose else's do you think?" replied the woman. "He isn't likely to take cold without 'em, I dare say."

"I hope he didn't die of anything catching? Eh?" said old Joe, stopping in his work, and looking up.

"What do you call this?" said Joe. "Bed-curtains!"

"Don't you be afraid of that," returned the woman. "I an't so fond of his company that I'd loiter about him for such things, if he did. Ah! you may look through that shirt till your eyes ache, but you won't find a hole in it, nor a threadbare place. It's the best he had, and a fine one too. They'd have wasted it, if it hadn't been for me."

"What do you call wasting of it?" asked old Joe.

"Putting it on him to be buried in, to be sure," replied the woman with a laugh. "Somebody was fool enough to do it, but I took it off again. If calico an't good enough for such a purpose, it isn't good enough for anything. It's quite as becoming to the body. He can't look uglier than he did in that one."

Scrooge listened to this dialogue in horror. As they sat grouped about their spoil, in the scanty light afforded by the old man's lamp, he viewed them with a detestation and disgust, which could hardly have been greater, though they had been obscene demons, marketing the corpse itself.

"Ha, ha!" laughed the same woman when old Joe, producing a flannel bag with money in it, told out their several gains upon the ground. "This is the end of it, you see! He frightened every one away from him when he was alive, to profit us when he was dead! Ha, ha, ha!"

"Spirit!" said Scrooge, shuddering from head to foot. "I see, I see. The case of this unhappy man might be my own. My life tends that way, now. Merciful heaven, what is this!"

He recoiled in terror, for the scene had changed, and now he almost touched a bed—a bare, uncurtained bed—on which, beneath a ragged sheet, there lay a something covered up, which, though it was dumb, announced itself in awful language.

The room was very dark, too dark to be observed with any accuracy, though Scrooge glanced round it in obedience to a secret impulse, anxious to know what kind of room it was. A pale light, rising in the outer air, fell straight upon the bed; and on it, plundered and bereft, unwatched, unwept, uncared for, was the body of this man.

Scrooge glanced towards the Phantom. Its steady hand was pointed to the head. The cover was so carelessly adjusted that the slightest raising of it, the motion of a finger upon Scrooge's part, would have disclosed the face. He thought of it, felt how easy it would be to do, and longed to do it; but had no more power to withdraw the veil than to dismiss the spectre at his side.

Oh cold, cold, rigid, dreadful Death, set up thine altar here, and dress it with such terrors as thou hast at thy command; for this is thy dominion! But of the loved, revered, and honoured head thou canst not turn one hair to thy dread purposes, or make one feature odious. It is not that the hand is heavy and will fall down when released; it is not that the heart and pulse are still; but that the hand was open, generous, and true; the heart brave, warm, and tender; and the

He had no more power to withdraw the veil
than to dismiss the spectre at his side.

pulse a man's. Strike, Shadow, strike! And see his good deeds springing from the wound, to sow the world with life immortal!

No voice pronounced these words in Scrooge's ears, and yet he heard them when he looked upon the bed. He thought, if this man could be raised up now, what would be his foremost thoughts? Avarice, hard-dealing, griping cares? They have brought him to a rich end, truly!

He lay, in the dark empty house, with not a man, a woman, or a child, to say that he was kind to me in this or that, and for the memory of one kind word I will be kind to him. A cat was tearing at the door, and there was a sound of gnawing rats beneath the hearth-stone. What *they* wanted in the room of death, and why they were so restless and disturbed, Scrooge did not dare to think.

"Spirit!" he said, "this is a fearful place. In leaving it, I shall not leave its lesson, trust me. Let us go!"

Still the Ghost pointed with an unmoved finger to the head.

"I understand you," Scrooge returned, "and I would do it if I could. But I have not the power, Spirit. I have not the power."

Again it seemed to look upon him.

"If there is any person in the town who feels emotion caused by this man's death," said Scrooge quite agonised, "show that person to me, Spirit, I beseech you!"

The Phantom spread its dark robe before him for a moment, like a wing; and withdrawing it, revealed a room by daylight, where a mother and her children were.

She was expecting some one, and with anxious eagerness; for she walked up and down the room; started at every sound; looked out from the window; glanced at the clock; tried, but in vain, to work with her needle; and could hardly bear the voices of the children in their play.

At length the long-expected knock was heard. She hurried to the door, and met her husband; a man whose face was care-worn and depressed, though he was young. There was a remarkable expression in it now; a kind of serious delight of which he felt ashamed, and which he struggled to repress.

He sat down to the dinner that had been hoarding for him by the fire; and when she asked him faintly what news (which was not until after a long silence), he appeared embarrassed how to answer.

"Is it good," she said, "or bad?"—to help him.

"Bad," he answered.

"We are quite ruined?"

"No. There is hope yet, Caroline."

"If *he* relents," she said, amazed, "there is! Nothing is past hope, if such a miracle has happened."

"He is past relenting," said her husband. "He is dead."

She was a mild and patient creature if her face spoke truth; but she was thankful in her soul to hear it, and she said so, with clasped hands. She prayed forgiveness the next moment, and was sorry; but the first was the emotion of her heart.

"What the half-drunken woman whom I told you of last night, said to me, when I tried to see him and obtain a week's delay; and what I thought was a mere excuse to avoid me; turns out to have been quite true. He was not only very ill, but dying, then."

"To whom will our debt be transferred?"

"I don't know. But before that time we shall be ready with the money; and even though we were not, it would be bad fortune indeed to find so merciless a creditor in his successor. We may sleep tonight with light hearts, Caroline!"

Yes. Soften it as they would, their hearts were lighter. The children's faces, hushed and clustered round to hear what they so little understood, were brighter; and it was a happier house for this man's death! The only emotion that the Ghost could show him, caused by the event, was one of pleasure.

"Let me see some tenderness connected with a death," said Scrooge; "or that dark chamber, Spirit, which we left just now, will be for ever present to me."

The Ghost conducted him through several streets familiar to his feet; and as they went along, Scrooge looked here and there to find himself, but nowhere was he to be seen. They entered poor Bob Cratchit's house; the dwelling he had visited before; and found the mother and the children seated round the fire.

Quiet. Very quiet. The noisy little Cratchits were as still as statues in one corner, and sat looking up at Peter, who had a book before him. The mother and her daughters were engaged in sewing. But surely they were very quiet!

" 'And He took a child, and set him in the midst of them.'[1] "

Where had Scrooge heard those words? He had not

dreamed them. The boy must have read them out, as he and the Spirit crossed the threshold. Why did he not go on?

The mother laid her work upon the table, and put her hand up to her face.

"The colour hurts my eyes," she said.

The colour? Ah, poor Tiny Tim![2]

"They're better now again," said Cratchit's wife. "It makes them weak by candle-light; and I wouldn't show weak eyes to your father when he comes home, for the world. It must be near his time."

"Past it rather," Peter answered, shutting up his book. "But I think he's walked a little slower than he used, these few last evenings, mother."

They were very quiet again. At last she said, and in a steady, cheerful voice, that only faultered once:

"I have known him walk with—I have known him walk with Tiny Tim upon his shoulder very fast indeed."

"And so have I!" cried Peter. "Often."

1　出自《聖經·馬可福音》第九章第36節。
2　指黑色，因為小提姆過世了，他們在縫製喪服。

"And so have I!" exclaimed another. So had all.

"But he was very light to carry," she resumed, intent upon her work, "and his father loved him so, that it was no trouble, no trouble. And there is your father at the door!"

She hurried out to meet him; and little Bob in his comforter—he had need of it, poor fellow—came in. His tea was ready for him on the hob, and they all tried who should help him to it most. Then the two young Cratchits got upon his knees and laid, each child a little cheek, against his face, as if they said, "Don't mind it, father. Don't be grieved!"

Bob was very cheerful with them, and spoke pleasantly to all the family. He looked at the work upon the table, and praised the industry and speed of Mrs. Cratchit and the girls. They would be done long before Sunday, he said.

"Sunday! You went today then, Robert?" said his wife.

"Yes, my dear," returned Bob. "I wish you could have gone. It would have done you good to see how green a place it is. But you'll see it often. I promised him that I would walk there on a Sunday. My little, little child!" cried Bob. "My little child!"

He broke down all at once. He couldn't help it. If he could have helped it, he and his child would have been farther apart perhaps than they were.

He left the room, and went upstairs into the room above, which was lighted cheerfully, and hung with Christmas. There was a chair set close beside the child, and there were signs of some one having been there lately. Poor Bob sat down in it, and when he had thought a little and composed himself, he kissed the little face. He was reconciled to what had happened, and went down again quite happy.

They drew about the fire, and talked; the girls and mother working still. Bob told them of the extraordinary kindness of Mr. Scrooge's nephew, whom he had scarcely seen but once, and who, meeting him in the street that day, and seeing that he looked a little—"just a little down you know," said Bob, inquired what had happened to distress him. "On which," said Bob, "for he is the pleasantest-spoken gentleman you ever heard, I told him. 'I am heartily sorry for it, Mr. Cratchit,' he said, 'and heartily sorry for your good wife.' By the bye, how he ever knew *that* I don't know."

"Knew what, my dear?"

"Why, that you were a good wife," replied Bob.

"Everybody knows that!" said Peter.

"Very well observed, my boy!" cried Bob. "I hope they do. 'Heartily sorry,' he said, 'for your good wife. If I can be of service to you in any way,' he said, giving me his card, 'that's where I live. Pray come to me.' Now, it wasn't," cried Bob, "for the sake of anything he might be able to do for us, so much as for his kind way, that this was quite delightful. It really seemed as if he had known our Tiny Tim, and felt with us."

"I'm sure he's a good soul!" said Mrs. Cratchit.

"You would be surer of it, my dear," returned Bob, "if you saw and spoke to him. I shouldn't be at all surprised, mark what I say, if he got Peter a better situation."

"Only hear that, Peter," said Mrs. Cratchit.

"And then," cried one of the girls, "Peter will be keeping company with some one, and setting up for himself."

"Get along with you!" retorted Peter, grinning.

"It's just as likely as not," said Bob, "one of these days; though there's plenty of time for that, my dear. But however and whenever we part from one another, I am sure we shall none of us forget poor Tiny Tim—shall we—or this first parting that there was among us?"

"Never, father!" cried they all.

"And I know," said Bob, "I know, my dears, that when we recollect how patient and how mild he was; although he was a little, little child; we shall not quarrel easily among ourselves, and forget poor Tiny Tim in doing it."

"No, never, father!" they all cried again.

"I am very happy," said little Bob, "I am very happy!"

Mrs. Cratchit kissed him, his daughters kissed him, the two young Cratchits kissed him, and Peter and himself shook hands. Spirit of Tiny Tim, thy childish essence was from God!

"Spectre," said Scrooge, "something informs me that our parting moment is at hand. I know it, but I know not how. Tell me what man that was whom we saw lying dead?"

The Ghost of Christmas Yet To Come conveyed him, as before—though at a different time, he thought: indeed, there seemed no order in these latter visions, save that they were in the Future—into the resorts of business men, but showed him not himself. Indeed, the Spirit did not stay for anything, but went straight on, as to the end just now desired, until besought by Scrooge to tarry for a moment.

"This court," said Scrooge, "through which we hurry now, is where my place of occupation is, and has been for a length of time. I see the house. Let me behold what I shall be, in days to come!"

The Spirit stopped; the hand was pointed elsewhere.

"The house is yonder," Scrooge exclaimed. "Why do you point away?"

The inexorable finger underwent no change.

Scrooge hastened to the window of his office, and looked in. It was an office still, but not his. The furniture was not the same, and the figure in the chair was not himself. The Phantom pointed as before.

He joined it once again, and wondering why and whither he had gone, accompanied it until they reached an iron gate. He paused to look round before entering.

A churchyard. Here, then the wretched man whose name he had now to learn, lay underneath the ground. It was a worthy place. Walled in by houses; overrun by grass and weeds, the growth of vegetation's death, not life; choked up with too much burying; fat with repleted appetite. A worthy place!

The Spirit stood among the graves, and pointed down to One. He advanced towards it trembling. The Phantom was exactly as it had been, but he dreaded that he saw new meaning in its solemn shape.

"Before I draw nearer to that stone to which you point," said Scrooge, "answer me one question. Are these the shadows of the things that Will be, or are they shadows of things that May be only?"

Still the Ghost pointed downward to the grave by which it stood.

"Men's courses will foreshadow certain ends, to which, if persevered in, they must lead," said Scrooge. "But if the courses be departed from, the ends will change. Say it is thus with what you show me!"

The Spirit was immovable as ever.

Scrooge crept towards it, trembling as he went; and following the finger, read upon the stone of the neglected grave his own name, EBENEZER SCROOGE.

"Am *I* that man who lay upon the bed?" he cried, upon his knees.

The finger pointed from the grave to him, and back again.

"No, Spirit! Oh no, no!"

The finger still was there.

"No, Spirit! Oh no, no!"

"Spirit!" he cried, tight clutching at its robe, "hear me! I am not the man I was. I will not be the man I must have been but for this intercourse. Why show me this, if I am past all hope?"

For the first time the hand appeared to shake.

"Good Spirit," he pursued, as down upon the ground he fell before it, "Your nature intercedes for me, and pities me. Assure me that I yet may change these shadows you have shown me, by an altered life!"

The kind hand trembled.

"I will honour Christmas in my heart, and try to keep it all the year. I will live in the Past, the Present, and the Future. The Spirits of all Three shall strive within me. I will not shut out the lessons that they teach. Oh, tell me I may sponge away the writing on this stone!"

In his agony, he caught the spectral hand. It sought to free itself, but he was strong in his entreaty, and detained it. The Spirit stronger yet, repulsed him.

Holding up his hands in a last prayer to have his fate reversed, he saw an alteration in the Phantom's hood and dress. It shrunk, collapsed, and dwindled down into a bed-post.

Stave Five

The End of It

Yes! and the bedpost was his own. The bed was his own, the room was his own. Best and happiest of all, the Time before him was his own, to make amends in!

"I will live in the Past, the Present, and the Future!" Scrooge repeated, as he scrambled out of bed. "The Spirits of all Three shall strive within me. Oh Jacob Marley! Heaven and the Christmas Time be praised for this! I say it on my knees, old Jacob; on my knees!"

He was so fluttered and so glowing with his good intentions, that his broken voice would scarcely answer to his call. He had been sobbing violently in his conflict with the Spirit, and his face was wet with tears.

"They are not torn down," cried Scrooge, folding one of his bed-curtains in his arms, "they are not torn down, rings and all. They are here—I am here—the

shadows of the things that would have been may be dispelled. They will be. I know they will!"

His hands were busy with his garments all this time: turning them inside out, putting them on upside down, tearing them, mislaying them, making them parties to every kind of extravagance.

"I don't know what to do!" cried Scrooge, laughing and crying in the same breath; and making a perfect Laocoön[1] of himself with his stockings. "I am as light as a feather, I am as happy as an angel, I am as merry

---

1　希臘神話人物，為特洛伊城的祭司，因警告特洛伊人勿中木馬計而觸怒天神，之後與兩個兒子遭海中巨蟒纏死。

as a school boy. I am as giddy as a drunken man. A merry Christmas to everybody! A happy New Year to all the world! Hallo here! Whoop! Hallo!"

He had frisked into the sitting-room, and was now standing there, perfectly winded.

"There's the saucepan that the gruel was in!" cried Scrooge, starting off again, and frisking round the fire-place. "There's the door, by which the Ghost of Jacob Marley entered! There's the corner where the Ghost of Christmas Present sat! There's the window where I saw the wandering Spirits! It's all right, it's all true, it all happened. Ha, ha, ha!"

Really, for a man who had been out of practice for so many years, it was a splendid laugh, a most illustrious laugh. The father of a long, long line of brilliant laughs!

"I don't know what day of the month it is!" said Scrooge. "I don't know how long I've been among the Spirits. I don't know anything. I'm quite a baby. Never mind. I don't care. I'd rather be a baby. Hallo! Whoop! Hallo here!"

He was checked in his transports by the churches ringing out the lustiest peals he had ever heard. Clash, clang, hammer, ding, dong, bell. Bell, dong, ding, hammer, clang, clash! Oh, glorious, glorious!

Running to the window, he opened it, and put out his head. No fog, no mist; clear, bright, jovial, stirring, cold; cold, piping for the blood to dance to; golden sunlight; heavenly sky; sweet fresh air; merry bells. Oh, glorious. Glorious!

"What's today!" cried Scrooge, calling downward to a boy in Sunday clothes, who perhaps had loitered in to look about him.

"EH?" returned the boy with all his might of wonder.

"What's today, my fine fellow?" said Scrooge.

"Today!" replied the boy. "Why, CHRISTMAS DAY"

"It's Christmas Day!" said Scrooge to himself. "I haven't missed it. The Spirits have done it all in one night. They can do anything they like. Of course they can. Of course they can. Hallo, my fine fellow!"

"Hallo!" returned the boy.

"Do you know the poulterer's, in the next street but one, at the corner?" Scrooge inquired.

"I should hope I did," replied the lad.

"An intelligent boy!" said Scrooge. "A remarkable boy! Do you know whether they've sold the prize Turkey that was hanging up there? Not the little prize

SCROOGE at the WINDOW.

"What's to-day, my fine
fellow?" said Scrooge.
"To-day!" replied the boy.
"Why, Christmas Day."

"What's today, my fine fellow?" said Scrooge.

Turkey: the big one?"

"What, the one as big as me?" returned the boy.

"What a delightful boy!" said Scrooge. "It's a pleasure to talk to him. Yes, my buck!"

"It's hanging there now," replied the boy.

"Is it?" said Scrooge. "Go and buy it."

"Walk-ER!" exclaimed the boy.

"No, no," said Scrooge, "I am in earnest. Go and buy it, and tell 'em to bring it here, that I may give them the direction where to take it. Come back with the man, and I'll give you a shilling. Come back with him in less than five minutes, and I'll give you half-a-crown!"

The boy was off like a shot. He must have had a steady hand at a trigger who could have got a shot off half so fast.

"I'll send it to Bob Cratchit's!" whispered Scrooge, rubbing his hands and splitting with a laugh. "He shan't know who sends it. It's twice the size of Tiny Tim. Joe Miller[2] never made such a joke as sending it to Bob's will be!"

2　Joe Miller（1684–1738），英國十八世紀的知名喜劇演員。1739年，John Mottley 假這位喜劇演員之名，編輯了一本笑話集，後來引申用來比喻老掉牙的笑話。

The hand in which he wrote the address was not a steady one, but write it he did, somehow, and went down stairs to open the street door, ready for the coming of the Poulterer's man. As he stood there, waiting his arrival, the knocker caught his eye.

"I shall love it, as long as I live!" cried Scrooge, patting it with his hand. "I scarcely ever looked at it before. What an honest expression it has in its face! It's a wonderful knocker!—Here's the Turkey. Hallo! Whoop! How are you! Merry Christmas!"

It was a Turkey! He never could have stood upon his legs, that bird. He would have snapped 'em short off in a minute, like sticks of sealing-wax.

"Why, it's impossible to carry that to Camden Town," said Scrooge. "You must have a cab."

The chuckle with which he said this, and the chuckle with which he paid for the Turkey, and the chuckle with which he paid for the cab, and the chuckle with which he recompensed the boy, were only to be exceeded by the chuckle with which he sat down breathless in his chair again, and chuckled till he cried.

Shaving was not an easy task, for his hand continued to shake very much; and shaving requires

Here's the Turkey. Hallo! Whoop!
How are you! Merry Christmas!

attention, even when you don't dance while you are at it. But if he had cut the end of his nose off, he would have put a piece of sticking-plaister over it, and been quite satisfied.

He dressed himself "all in his best," and at last got out into the streets. The people were by this time pouring forth, as he had seen them with the Ghost of Christmas Present; and walking with his hands behind him, Scrooge regarded every one with a delighted smile.

He looked so irresistibly pleasant, in a word, that three or four good-humoured fellows said, "Good morning, sir! A merry Christmas to you!" And Scrooge said often afterwards, that of all the blithe sounds he had ever heard, those were the blithest in his ears.

He had not gone far, when coming on towards him he beheld the portly gentleman, who had walked into his counting-house the day before and said, "Scrooge and Marley's, I believe?" It sent a pang across his heart to think how this old gentleman would look upon him when they met; but he knew what path lay straight before him, and he took it.

"My dear sir," said Scrooge, quickening his pace, and taking the old gentleman by both his hands. "How

Scrooge regarded every one with a delighted smile.

do you do? I hope you succeeded yesterday. It was very kind of you. A merry Christmas to you, sir!"

"Mr. Scrooge?"

"Yes," said Scrooge. "That is my name, and I fear it may not be pleasant to you. Allow me to ask your pardon. And will you have the goodness"—here Scrooge whispered in his ear.

"Lord bless me!" cried the gentleman, as if his breath were gone. "My dear Mr. Scrooge, are you serious?"

"If you please," said Scrooge. "Not a farthing less. A great many back-payments are included in it, I assure you. Will you do me that favour?"

"My dear sir," said the other, shaking hands with him. "I don't know what to say to such munifi—"

"Don't say anything, please," retorted Scrooge. "Come and see me. Will you come and see me?"

"I will!" cried the old gentleman. And it was clear he meant to do it.

"Thank'ee," said Scrooge. "I am much obliged to you. I thank you fifty times. Bless you!"

He went to church, and walked about the streets, and watched the people hurrying to and fro, and patted children on the head, and questioned beggars, and looked down into the kitchens of houses, and up to the windows; and found that everything could yield him pleasure. He had never dreamed that any walk—that anything—could give him so much happiness. In the afternoon he turned his steps towards his nephew's house.

He passed the door a dozen times, before he had the courage to go up and knock. But he made a dash and did it.

"Is your master at home, my dear?" said Scrooge to the girl. Nice girl! Very.

"Yes, sir."

"Where is he, my love?" said Scrooge.

"He's in the dining-room, sir, along with mistress. I'll show you up stairs, if you please."

"Thank'ee. He knows me," said Scrooge, with his hand already on the dining-room lock. "I'll go in here, my dear."

He turned it gently, and sidled his face in, round the door. They were looking at the table (which was spread out in great array); for these young housekeepers are always nervous on such points, and like to see that everything is right.

"Fred!" said Scrooge.

Dear heart alive, how his niece by marriage started! Scrooge had forgotten, for the moment, about her sitting in the corner with the footstool, or he wouldn't have done it, on any account.

"Why bless my soul!" cried Fred, "who's that?"

"It's I. Your uncle Scrooge. I have come to dinner. Will you let me in, Fred?"

Let him in! It is a mercy he didn't shake his arm off. He was at home in five minutes. Nothing could be heartier. His niece looked just the same. So did Topper when *he* came. So did the plump sister, when *she* came. So did every one when they came. Wonderful party, wonderful games, wonderful unanimity, won-der-ful happiness!

But he was early at the office next morning. Oh, he was early there. If he could only be there first, and catch Bob Cratchit coming late! That was the thing he had set his heart upon.

And he did it; yes he did! The clock struck nine. No Bob. A quarter past. No Bob. He was full eighteen minutes and a half, behind his time. Scrooge sat with his door wide open, that he might see him come into the tank.

His hat was off before he opened the door; his

"It's I. Your uncle Scrooge. I have come to dinner.
Will you let me in, Fred?"

comforter too. He was on his stool in a jiffy; driving away with his pen, as if he were trying to overtake nine o'clock.

"Hallo!" growled Scrooge, in his accustomed voice as near as he could feign it. "What do you mean by coming here at this time of day?"

"I am very sorry, sir," said Bob. "I *am* behind my time."

"You are?" repeated Scrooge. "Yes. I think you are. Step this way, if you please."

"It's only once a year, sir," pleaded Bob, appearing from the tank. "It shall not be repeated. I was making rather merry yesterday, sir."

"Now, I'll tell you what, my friend," said Scrooge, "I am not going to stand this sort of thing any longer. And therefore," he continued, leaping from his stool, and giving Bob such a dig in the waistcoat that he staggered back into the tank again: "and therefore I am about to raise your salary!"

Bob trembled, and got a little nearer to the ruler. He had a momentary idea of knocking Scrooge down with it; holding him; and calling to the people in the court for help and a strait-waistcoat.

"A merry Christmas, Bob!" said Scrooge, with an

I am about to raise your salary!

earnestness that could not be mistaken, as he clapped him on the back. "A merrier Christmas, Bob, my good fellow, than I have given you, for many a year! I'll raise your salary, and endeavour to assist your struggling family, and we will discuss your affairs this very afternoon, over a Christmas bowl of smoking bishop, Bob! Make up the fires, and buy another coal-scuttle before you dot another i[3], Bob Cratchit!"

Scrooge was better than his word. He did it all, and infinitely more; and to Tiny Tim, who did NOT die, he was a second father. He became as good a friend, as good a master, and as good a man, as the good old city knew, or any other good old city, town, or borough, in the good old world.

Some people laughed to see the alteration in him, but he let them laugh, and little heeded them; for he was wise enough to know that nothing ever happened on this globe, for good, at which some people did not have their fill of laughter in the outset; and knowing that such as these would be blind anyway, he thought

---

3 指「dot the i's and cross the t's」，意思是「對細節一絲不苟」。dot 是「打圓點」，cros是「畫橫線」。「dot the i's and cross the t's」就 是說，寫「i」的時候要加一點，寫「t」的時候要畫一橫線。

I'll raise your salary.

it quite as well that they should wrinkle up their eyes in grins, as have the malady in less attractive forms. His own heart laughed, and that was quite enough for him.

He had no further intercourse with Spirits, but lived upon the Total Abstinence Principle[4], ever afterwards; and it was always said of him that he knew how to keep Christmas well, if any man alive possessed the knowledge. May that be truly said of us, and all of us! And so, as Tiny Tim observed, God Bless Us, Every One!

4　spirit 有「幽靈」之意，也有「酒精」之意。「不和幽靈打交道」和「不沾染酒精」有雙關語的趣味。

小氣財神

第一樂章

馬里的鬼魂

P. 6 　　故事一開始要先說的是，馬里已經作古了，這是不容置疑的，牧師、教堂執事、葬儀社人員、喪家代表，都在葬禮登記簿上簽了名。史古基也簽了名。史古基的簽名在交易所[1]是很管用的，只要他肯抬起貴手簽名。老馬里已經掛了，「就像釘死在門上的門釘一樣」[2]。

　　請注意，這不是說我知道門釘和死亡有什麼特別的關連。我個人是覺得，棺材釘才是五金行裡面和死亡最有關連的東西。不過，這個譬喻裡面有我們老祖先的智慧，不容我不潔的雙手去竄改，亂了社會綱紀。是故，容我再強調一次：老馬里已經掛了，就像釘死在門上的門釘一樣。

1　指當時倫敦的皇家交易所（Royal Exchange）。
2　英文「as dead as a doornail」，這是莎士比亞時代常見的譬喻法。

P.7　史古基知道他已經魂歸西天了嗎？當然知道，怎麼會不知道呢？兩人合夥都不知多少年了。而且史古基還是他唯一的遺囑執行人、遺產管理人、財產受讓人、遺產繼承人，也是唯一的友人、唯一來送殯的人。不過史古基並沒有被這件

耶柏尼澤·史古基

憾事所擊垮，葬禮當天，他展現了生意人的本色，以極低的費用，隆重地舉辦了葬禮。

　　講到馬里的葬禮，回到我開宗明義提到的：馬里已經作古了，這是不容置疑的。這一定要交代清楚，不然我接下來要講的故事就沒什麼奇特之處。這就好比我們如果沒有徹底明白哈姆雷特的父王在戲劇開演之前就已經駕崩，那麼——他在一個吹著東風的夜裡，來到王宮的城牆上蹓躂，去嚇嚇自己那個怯懦的兒子——這樣的事就沒什麼好稀奇的了。那充其量就是有個中年紳士，天黑後去了某個有風的地方，譬如聖保羅教堂的墓地，然後突然在那裡現身罷了。

P.8　史古基一直沒有把老馬里的姓氏塗掉，幾年過去

了，矗立在店門口上方的招牌依舊寫著「史古基與馬里」。公司的商號就叫作「史古基與馬里」，剛入業界的新手，有人會對著史古基叫史古基，也有人會叫他馬里，史古基都會應聲，反正對他來說都一樣。

哦！這史古基啊，是個死不鬆手的鐵公雞！他是個壓榨、豪取、強奪、剝削、攫取、貪婪的老惡棍！他像打火石那樣又硬又尖，沒有鋼鐵能在上面打出火花。他行事隱密，封閉又孤僻。他內心冷酷，冰凍了垂老的外表。他的尖鼻子被凍傷，臉頰乾癟，走路步伐僵硬，眼睛發紅，薄薄的嘴唇泛著青色，用刺耳的聲音講出精明的話。他的頭部、眉毛、瘦削的下巴，都結著白霜。他總是帶著一身的寒氣，使得他的辦公室在三伏天也能結冰，在聖誕時節更別指望溫度能上升個一度。

史古基對天氣的冷熱，不痛不癢。天熱，他不感到溫暖；天冷，也不感到寒冷。他這個人比寒風更刺骨，比大雪更不肯罷手，比暴雨更不饒人。惡劣的天氣也對他莫可奈何，暴雨狂雪、冰雹凍雨唯一能夠誇口勝過他的地方，就是它們時常「出手」大方，但是史古基不幹這種事。

P.9 在街上，沒有人會開心地叫住他，「親愛的史古基，最近好嗎？什麼時候來我家坐坐？」沒有乞丐會跟他要一點施捨，沒有小孩會去問他現在幾點了，甚至他這輩子都還沒有人來跟他問過路。盲人的狗也認得他，只要看到他走過來，就會把主人拉進門或是拉進巷子裡，然後搖搖尾巴，像是在說：「失明的主人啊！與其長著邪惡的眼睛，不如沒有眼睛！」

P. 10　　那麼，史古基在乎什麼呢？他恰恰就喜歡這樣！在史古基看來——在熙攘的人生道路上，一邊擠身前進，一邊還要警告人情滾遠一點——這不就是智者們所說的傻子嘛。

　　曾有個聖誕夜，這是一年中最美好的日子。老史古基坐在帳房裡忙著，天氣寒冷刺骨，霧氣瀰漫，外面巷道上傳來人們來來往往、氣喘吁吁的聲音，人們用手拍打胸部，在石板地上踩腳，想讓自己暖和些。城裡的時鐘才剛敲過三點，天色就已經暗了，雖說今天一整天也未見明亮過。附近幾間辦公室的窗內已經燭火搖曳，看起來像是在暗色的空氣上蘸著紅點。霧氣從每一道裂縫、每一個鑰匙孔，灌進屋子裡。外頭霧氣濃密，連在最狹小的巷弄裡，對面的房子看起來也像是幢幢幻影。看著陰暗的濃霧籠罩下來，眼前一片朦朧，會以為自然之神就住在附近，而且正在滾煮著一大鍋水。

P. 13　　史古基讓帳房的門敞開，以便監視公司的文書員

老史古基坐在帳房裡忙著

人員，文書員正在另一邊只有櫥櫃般大小的陰暗隔間裡抄寫信件。史古基生的爐火很小，文書員的爐火更小，看起來只有一塊煤炭，但是他不能加煤炭，因為史古基把煤炭箱放在自己的辦公間裡。要是他拿著鏟子走進去，老闆一定會說他們無法再共事了。文書員只好圍上白色的長圍巾，想藉著燭火取暖，不過他不是什麼想像力豐富的人，所以也起不了什麼作用。

「舅舅，聖誕快樂！上帝拯救你！」一個愉快的聲音叫喊著。那是史古基的外甥，他快步走過來，話才一說完，人就來到史古基的面前了。

「呸！鬼扯淡！」史古基說。

外甥剛剛在霜霧中快步疾走來讓身子暖和，現在整個人容光煥發，氣色紅潤，眼睛炯炯有神，呼氣又吐出了白煙。

P. 15 「舅舅，你說聖誕節是鬼扯淡？你不是這個意思吧，對不對？」外甥說道。

「我就是這個意思。」史古基說：「聖誕快樂！你有什麼權利快樂？有什麼理由快樂？你都夠窮了。」

外甥語氣愉快地回答：「那你又有什麼權利不高興？有什麼理由悶悶不樂？你已經夠有錢了。」

史古基一時不知如何回答，又「呸」了一次，說

213

「舅舅，聖誕快樂！上帝拯救你！」
愉快的聲音叫喊著。

「鬼扯淡」！

「別生氣了，舅舅！」外甥說道。

史古基說：「我還能怎樣？我活在這樣一個都是傻瓜的世界裡。聖誕快樂！有什麼好快樂的！對你來說，聖誕節不就是這樣的日子：要付帳單卻沒錢付，發現自己又老了一歲，卻沒有一刻過過有錢人的生活；在結算帳簿時，發現整年十二個月的每一條帳目，都在找你的麻煩。」史古基氣呼呼地說：「要是由我來作主，每一個到處講『聖誕快樂』的蠢蛋，都應該和他自己的布丁一起蒸了，在心臟插上冬青樹枝，然後埋了。就應該這樣！」

P. 16　「舅舅！」外甥哀求道。

史古基用嚴厲的語氣說：「外甥，你過你的聖誕節，我過我的！」

「你過你的聖誕節！」史古基的外甥重複他的話說：「你又不過聖誕節！」

「那就隨便我吧。」史古基說：「希望過節能帶給你好處！聖誕節都有帶給你好處吧！」

外甥回答說：「我敢說，有很多事情都讓我可以從中得到好處，但不是從中得到利益，譬如聖誕節就是這樣。姑且不說聖誕節的神聖名稱和起源有多麼令人崇

「那就隨便我吧。」史古基說。

敬，每當聖誕節快到的時候，我就會想聖誕節真是殊勝，是一個仁慈、寬恕、慷慨、快樂的時節。就我知道的，一個年頭裡也就只有這麼一天，男男女女都會贊同應該要敞開緊閉的心胸，將那些生活不如自己的人，當作是人生旅途上一輩子的同行夥伴，而不是將他們看成是非我族類，各走各的路。所以，舅舅，雖然聖誕節不曾在我的口袋裡放進一點金子或銀子，但是聖誕節已經帶給了我好處，以後也會繼續帶給我好處。所以我要說，願上帝保佑這個佳節！」

P.18　櫥櫃裡的文書員聽了，不禁拍手鼓掌，不過隨即又意識到自己失態了。他撥了撥火堆，卻把最後那一點微弱的火光給弄熄了。

史古基說：「你要是敢再出聲音，就捲鋪蓋回家過節。」他轉向外甥，又說：「先生，你真是能言善道，我好奇你怎麼不進去國會當議員。」

「舅舅，請息怒。明天過來跟我們一起吃飯吧！」

史古基說，他倒想先看他……[3]——沒錯，他真的脫口說了整句詛咒的話，然後又說他要是先嗝屁了，他

3　未講完的詛咒語，完整語為「see him go to the devil first」，指「想先看他去死」。

就會去看他。

「哪會？哪會啊？」外甥叫喊道。

「你怎麼結婚了？」[4]史古基問。

P. 19　「我愛上人家了呀。」

「你愛上人家了！」史古基咆哮道，彷彿世界上就這事比「聖誕快樂」更可笑。「慢走！」

「舅舅，別這樣。我還沒結婚的時候，你也沒來看我，何必拿這個當理由？」

「慢走。」史古基說。

「我沒有要圖你什麼，也沒有要跟你討什麼，我們怎麼就不能好好相處呢？」

「慢走。」史古基說。

「看到你這麼堅決，我心裡很難過。我們沒有吵過架，我也不會跟你吵。我盡力表現了對聖誕節的敬意，一直到聖誕節期間的最後一刻，我都會保持好心情。所以，舅舅，聖誕快樂！」

「慢走！」史古基說。

「也祝你新年快樂！」

4　指外甥沒有錢，卻敢結婚；而為愛情結婚，更是荒謬。

「慢走！」史古基回答。

史古基的外甥沒有發出一句惡言。他走出帳房，在外面的門口停下來，跟文書員說了祝賀佳節的話。文書員雖然渾身發冷，但還是比史古基溫暖多了，因為他熱情地回應了對方的問候。

P.20 「又是一個蠢蛋。」史古基無意中聽到文書員的談話後，喃喃自語道：「這個文書員，一個星期才賺十五先令，有老婆、有家庭，還跟人家說什麼『聖誕快樂』。我真是快瘋了。」

這個蠢蛋把史古基的外甥送出門後，又讓另外兩個訪客進了門。那是兩位體型壯碩的紳士，一副和藹可親的樣子，他們這時脫下帽子，站在史古基的辦公室裡，手裡拿著簿子和文件，向他鞠了躬。

「貴公司是『史古基與馬里』吧！」一位紳士看著手上的名單，說道：「我有這個榮幸和史古基先生或馬里先生說話嗎？」

「馬里先生已經過世七年了，就在七年前今天這個晚上過世的。」史古基回答說。

「我們相信，他的慷慨一定也能夠從他在世的合夥人身上展現出來。」紳士說道，一邊出示募款人證書。

這話倒是講的沒錯，兩個合夥人的個性很像。一

「我有這個榮幸和史古基先生或馬里先生說話嗎？」

聽到「慷慨」這個不祥的字眼，史古基就蹙眉搖頭，把證書遞了回去。

「史古基先生，在一年中這個歡樂的節日裡」，紳士拿起筆來，說道：「我們更應該布施，去救濟貧窮困苦的人，他們正飽受著飢寒之苦。有很多人生活匱乏，還有更多的人生活有待改善。」

P. 22　「監獄還有吧？」史古基問。

「還有很多。」紳士說著，把筆放了下來。

「那勞動救濟院⁵呢？還有在運作嗎？」史古基追問。

「還有。」紳士回答：「但願這些機構都關閉不再需要了。」

「所以磨坊法和濟貧法⁶都還在執行中？」史古基問。

「都還熱鬧滾滾地在執行中。」

「哦！剛剛聽你講，還以為發生什麼事，讓這些都停擺了。現在聽你這麼說，我就放心了。」史古基說。

5　勞動救濟院（workhouse），為貧弱之人提供住處和生計的機構。
6　《磨坊法》（Treadmill）是針對犯人，讓犯人踩踏車，有些並藉此產生動力，用來從事生產。《濟貧法》（Poor Law）用於勞動救濟院。

「但是這些措施並未讓人們的身心得到安穩。」紳士答道：「所以我們幾個人才會發起募款，幫窮人買一些肉品、飲料和取暖用品。我們之所以會選在這個時候來募款，是因為這是一年當中最歡樂卻也是需求最迫切的時刻。我要替您寫多少金額呢？」

P. 23　　「不用寫！」史古基回答。

　　「您是希望匿名嗎？」

　　「我希望你們離開。」史古基說：「兩位先生，既然你們問我的意願，這就是我的答案。我自己不過聖誕節，也不會花錢讓那些懶鬼去過聖誕節。剛才提的那些機構，我也出了一份力，他們耗費的錢已經夠多了，日子過不下去的人，就去那裡報到吧。」

　　「有很多人去不了，還有很多人是寧願死，也不願意去。」

　　「寧願死也不願意去，那就死吧，順便可以減少過剩的人口。還有……抱歉……這些我就不懂了。」史古基說。

　　「您可以了解看看。」紳士說道。

　　「那不關我的事。」史古基答道：「人管好自己就行了，不必去過問別人的事。我自己的事都忙不過來了。慢走了，兩位紳士！」

　　兩位紳士知道多說無益，就告退了。發表過高論之後，史古基回到工作上，心情顯得比平時愉快。

P.24　　這時，霧色漸濃，天色昏暗，有人拿著灼亮的火把跑來跑去、提供照明，在馬車前方為馬匹帶路。古老教堂的鐘樓上，鐘聲粗嘎的老鐘，透過牆上那扇哥德式的窗戶，悄悄地往下覷著史古基，但老鐘這時候隱沒不見，只聽得見濃霧中響起的整點和每一刻鐘的報時。鐘聲響後，餘音顫抖，就像牙齒在凍僵的頭顱裡打著冷顫，咯咯作響。

　　這時候，氣溫更低了，大街上的巷弄轉角處，有幾個工人在修理煤氣管。他們在炭盆裡生起大火，一群衣衫襤褸的男人和男孩圍了過來，開心地在炙熱的火光前烘著雙手、眨動眼睛。水龍頭被冷落在一旁，滲出來的水，冷不防的凍成了冰，對人類不懷好意。

　　明亮的商店裡，在櫥窗燈的熱度下，冬青的樹枝和果子生氣盎然，行人蒼白的臉被照得紅潤。賣雞鴨的和賣雜貨的，可壯觀有趣了，看起來就像一場好不熱鬧的慶典，真難想像還有喊價買賣這檔子事。

　　氣派的官邸裡，市長大人下令，要求五十名廚師和男僕，要讓聖誕節慶展現出官邸應有的派頭。就連那位小裁縫師，他上星期一才因為在街上酒醉鬧事，被罰了五先令，如今也在自己的閣樓裡攪拌著明天要吃的布丁，而他瘦巴巴的妻子，帶著小寶寶出門去買牛肉了。

P. 25 霧更濃，天也更冷了！寒氣逼人，凜冽刺骨。 當年，聖鄧斯坦如果不是用他慣用的武器[7]，而是用這樣的嚴寒來挾住魔鬼的鼻子，魔鬼也會冷得大吼大叫。酷寒咬囓著一個孩子小小的鼻子，就像狗啃咬著骨頭那樣，這孩子彎下腰，對著店門上的鑰匙孔唱著聖誕頌歌，想唱給史古基聽，但才一唱到——

快樂的先生，上帝祝福您！
祝您萬事如意！

P. 26 史古基就抓起一把尺，那種架勢嚇得唱歌的小孩逃之夭夭，鑰匙孔四周只剩濃霧，還有更顯得相襯的嚴霜。

好不容易，下班的時間到了。史古基不情願地從

---

7 聖鄧斯坦（St. Dunstan），十世紀左右的人物，曾是一名鐵匠。一日，惡魔化身來誘惑他，但是被他識破，他拿起一個燒紅的鐵鉗，挾住惡魔的鼻子，惡魔痛得唉唉大叫。

「不方便，也不合理。」史古基說

凳子上起來，這個動作默許了可以下班了。小隔間裡巴望著下班的文書員立刻熄滅燭火，戴上帽子。

「我猜你明天想請一整天的假吧？」史古基說。

「是的，如果方便的話，先生。」

「既不方便，也不合理。我要是因此扣掉你半克朗的薪水，你就會覺得不合理，我說得沒錯吧？」史古基說。

文書員微微笑了一下。

「不過，你不用來上班，我卻還得付你一天的薪水，你就不會覺得我虧大了！」史古基又說。

文書員表示，一年也就只有這麼一次而已。

「這是哪門子的理由，每年十二月二十五日，這樣竊取別人口袋裡的錢！」史古基一面說，一面把大衣的釦子扣到下巴，「我想你明天一定會請一整天假，後天早上要早一點到！」

文書員說自己一定會提早到。史古基大聲嚷著，一邊走出辦公室。辦公室隨即關上，文書員圍著白色的長圍巾垂到腰間（他沒有大衣可以穿）。他跟在一排男孩的後面，沿著康希爾的坡道往下滑了二十趟來慶祝聖誕夜。接著，他飛奔回肯頓鎮，準備回家玩捉迷藏。

P. 29　　史古基到他常去的沉悶飯館，吃了一頓沉悶的晚

文書員沿著康希爾的坡道往下滑

餐。他把報紙上的新聞都看遍了，接著把剩餘的時間拿來消磨在銀行帳冊上，然後回家睡覺。他現在住的地方，以前歸已故合夥人所有，房間陰陰暗暗的，位在一座庭院上方的一排陰暗建築裡。這排房子像是跑錯地方一樣，讓人禁不住想，房子在年少時一定是跟別的房子玩捉迷藏，躲到了這裡，卻忘了出去的路。如今這棟房子夠老舊了，也夠陰森了，只有史古基住在裡面，其他房間都租出去當辦公室了。庭院裡很陰暗，對這裡的每一塊石頭都瞭如指掌的史古基，也不得不摸索著前進。房子的黑色大門很老舊，四周瀰漫著濃霧寒霜，彷彿掌管氣候的神靈就坐在門檻上，哀傷地沉思著。

P. 30 　　到現在，要說的是，除了門上的門環特別大，其他沒有什麼特別的。另一件事是，打從史古基住進去之後，他每天早晚都會看到這個門環。此外，史古基就和倫敦市的任何一個人一樣（恕我斗膽，包括市府員工、市政官、公會成員）都是想像力貧乏的人。還有，還要記住的是：史古基今天下午提到過世七年的合夥人之後，他的腦海裡就沒再浮現過馬里。既然如此，當史古基把鑰匙插進鎖孔時，門環怎麼會無聲無息地突然變成馬里的臉？有誰能跟我解釋這種事嗎？

　　馬里的臉，不像院子裡其他東西那樣黑抹抹的一

門環變成馬里的臉

團陰影，而是散發著一圈昏暗的光，就像一隻放在陰暗地窖裡的腐壞龍蝦。馬里的臉不兇不惡，只是用他慣有的眼神盯著史古基看。他戴著一副鬼影幽幽的眼鏡，眼鏡架在鬼影幽幽的額頭上，一頭怪異的亂髮，像是被風或是熱氣給吹亂。他眼睛睜得斗大，眨也不眨，再加上一臉的青灰色，好不嚇人。不過，恐怖感卻不是來自於那張臉或是表情，而且那種恐怖感也不是那張臉可以控制的。

P. 32　史古基再定睛一看，幻象又變回了門環。

不能說他沒有嚇一跳，也不能說他的血液中沒有感受到一種從小未曾有過的恐怖感。但他還是把剛才縮回來的手放回鑰匙上，毅然地開了門，走進屋內，把蠟燭點亮。

但是在闔上門之前，他確實停頓、遲疑了一會兒。他先謹慎地查看了一下門的後方，好像期待會看到馬里的辮子伸進門廊來嚇他。然而，門後什麼也沒有，只有幾根釘住門環的螺絲釘和螺絲帽。他「呸」了兩聲，砰地把門關上。

關門的聲音像打雷一樣，響徹整棟房子。樓上的每個房間、樓下酒商的每個酒桶，各自轟轟作響。史古基不是那種會怕回聲的人。他把門鎖好，走過大廳，慢慢地走上樓，一邊修剪著燭蕊。

P. 33　　你可以含糊地說，有一輛六匹馬拉著的馬車，開上了一段老舊的樓梯，或是開進了一個漏洞百出的國會新法案[8]裡。但我其實要說的是，是可以把靈車橫著弄上樓梯，只需讓車頭的橫木頂著牆，車尾的門對著樓梯欄杆，這是輕而易舉就能辦得到的。樓梯很寬，空間夠大了。大概也因為這樣，在一片昏暗中，史古基會覺得自己看到了一輛靈車在眼前駛過。外面街上的幾盞煤氣燈連門口都照不亮，所以你可以想見史古基拿著燭火，光線會有多暗。

　　史古基繼續走上樓，不以為意。黑暗不用花錢，這很合史古基的意。不過，在關上厚重的臥室門之前，他還是先去各個房間看了看，確認沒有異狀，畢竟剛才那張臉鮮明猶新。

　　客廳、臥室、儲藏室，沒有異樣。桌子下面沒有人，沙發下面也沒有人；壁爐裡有微弱的火；湯匙和餐盤放置得好好的；壁爐擱架上有一小鍋燕麥粥（史古基有點著涼）。床底下沒有人，衣櫥裡沒有人，他掛在

8　諷刺當時英國議會通過的法案往往漏洞百出，讓人能夠輕易地鑽法律漏洞。

牆上的睡袍形狀有點奇怪，但裡頭也沒有人。儲藏室也沒有異樣，一樣是老舊的壁爐圍欄、舊鞋、兩個魚簍、一個三腳洗臉架和一把火鉗。

P. 34　檢查滿意後，他安心地關上房門，把自己鎖在裡面，上了兩道鎖，但這不是他平時的習慣。經過妥善防禦，以防什麼嚇人的事之後，他解下圍巾，穿上睡袍和拖鞋，戴上睡帽，然後坐在爐火前，吃起粥來。

那爐火真是微弱，在這樣的寒夜裡，沒什麼作用。他緊挨壁爐坐著，彎身傾在爐火上，才能從一小簇爐火中得到一絲暖意。壁爐很老舊，那是很久以前的荷蘭商人建造的，周圍鋪著古怪的荷蘭磁磚，講述著聖經的故事。有該隱和亞伯、法老王的女兒、希芭女王、從輕柔如羽毛床的雲端

下凡的天使信差、亞伯拉罕、伯沙撒、乘著奶油船航海的使徒們，有上百個圖案可以吸引他的注意，然而，馬里的那張臉，他都死了七年了，還像古代先知的法杖那樣，把眼前這些畫面都吞噬掉[9]。如果說這每一塊光滑的磁磚一開始就是空白的，而且有法力可以把他雜亂的念頭顯相出來，那麼每塊磁磚上都會映出一張張老馬里的臉。

P. 35 　　「鬼扯淡！」史古基說著，在房裡踱起步來。

　　走了幾趟後，他又坐下來，把頭仰靠在椅背上，視線剛好落在房間裡掛著的一個銅鈴上，銅鈴原本是為著某些不復記憶的原因，用來和公寓頂樓的房間連絡的，現在已經廢棄不用。他一看，大吃一驚，一陣說不出的恐懼感，因為他看見銅鈴開始晃動，一開始是輕微搖晃，沒有發出聲響，但不久開始大聲作響，屋子裡其他的銅鈴也都響了起來。

P. 36 　　這大概持續了半分鐘或一分鐘，但感覺像有一個鐘頭那麼久。銅鈴一起發出聲響，也同時安靜下來。接著，下方傳來一陣噹啷的聲響，聽起來像是有人拖著粗

9　出自《舊約聖經‧出埃及記》的典故：亞倫的手杖化成蛇，將其他人的手杖都吞噬掉。

史古基吃驚地看著銅鈴

重的鐵鍊，在酒商地窖裡的酒桶上走過。史古基這時想到，聽說在鬧鬼的房子裡，鬼就是拖著鐵鍊走的。

地窖的門砰地一聲被打開，接著他聽到樓下地板上的鐵鍊聲愈來愈大聲，接著聲音上了樓梯，直接朝他的房門過來。

「沒有這種鬼事！我才不信。」史古基說。

但他還是臉色大變，因為那東西沒有任何停頓，直接穿越厚重的房門進到房內，來到他的眼前。它一進來，原本快熄滅的火突然往上竄，好像在叫喊著：「我認得，那是馬里的鬼魂！」然後火焰又黯了下去。

P. 39 就是那張臉，絲毫不差。它紮著辮子，一身的背心、緊身褲、皮靴，那是馬里平時的穿著。皮靴上的流蘇，跟辮子、背心下擺、頭上的頭髮一樣，飄了起來。拖著的鐵鍊纏繞在腰間，鐵鍊很長，像條尾巴繞在身上。史古基仔細看了一下，鐵鍊上串著鋼鐵打造的現金箱、鑰匙、鎖頭、帳簿、契據和沉甸甸的錢包。他的身體是透明的，所以史古基看著他時，可以看穿他的背心，看到背心後面的兩顆鈕扣。

史古基以前常聽人家說馬里沒有心肝，他現在算是相信了。

「我認識他！那是馬里的鬼魂！」

不，他至今還是不肯相信。儘管他把鬼魂看了又看，鬼魂就立在眼前；儘管鬼魂死氣冰冷的眼神逼儡而來，一條打摺的方巾從鬼魂的頭頂繞到下巴綁住[10]；儘管他連方巾的材質都看得一清二楚（他之前沒注意到這條方巾），他還是滿腹狐疑，不肯相信自己親眼所見到的東西。

P.40 「怎麼！找我有什麼事？」史古基用刻薄冷酷的慣有語氣說。

「事情可多了！」那是馬里的聲音，不用懷疑。

「你是誰？」

「你應該問我『生前』是誰。」

「你『生前』是誰？」史古基提高音調說，「跟其他的鬼比起來，你很不一樣。」其實他本來是想說，「都做鬼了，你還真挑剔」，但他後來改口，感覺比較妥當。

「我生前是你的合夥人，雅各・馬里。」

「你能……能坐下嗎？」史古基問道，一臉懷疑地看著他。

---

10 在狄更斯的時代，會用方巾從死者的頭頂繞到下巴綁住，以防下巴脫開。

UPON its coming in the dying flame leaped up as though it cried, "I know him; Marley's Ghost!" and fell again.

「能。」

「那就坐下吧。」

史古基之所以這樣問，是因為不知這麼透明的鬼魂，能不能坐在椅子上。他覺得，鬼魂要是無法坐在椅子上，可能就要尷尬地解釋一番。不過，鬼魂在壁爐對面的椅子上坐下來，一副很習慣的樣子。

「你還是不相信。」鬼魂說道。

「不相信。」史古基說。

「除了親眼所見，你還需要什麼證據，才會相信我是真的存在？」

P. 43　「不知道。」史古基說道。

「你都親眼看到了，怎麼還懷疑？」

「只要一點小事，感官就會被干擾。胃有一點不舒服，感官就會被蒙蔽。你可能只是一小塊牛肉沒有消化掉，或是一點芥末、一小片乳酪或是一小塊沒煮熟的馬鈴薯而已。不管你是什麼，說你是從墳墓來的，不如說你是肉汁造成的！」史古基說。

史古基不愛開玩笑，也沒有那種閒情逸致。事實上，他想裝得機敏些，好分散自己的注意力，把恐懼感壓下來，因為鬼魂的聲音讓他毛骨悚然。

史古基覺得，只是這樣坐著，靜靜地瞪著對方呆滯不動的眼睛，對自己並不利。還有一件事情也很可怕，鬼魂渾身散發出陰間地府的氣息，這是真的，儘管史古基感受不到，因為鬼魂雖然紋風不動地坐著，但是頭髮、衣擺、流蘇一直飄動著，像是被爐子上的熱氣所吹動那樣。

「你有看到這根牙籤嗎？」史古基問。鑑於以上所述，他很快又出招，想讓鬼魂將動也不動的眼神從他身上移開，就算移開一下下也好。

P. 45　　「有看到。」鬼魂答道。

「你又沒在看！」史古基說。

「但我還是看到了。」鬼魂說。

「好吧，我乾脆把這根牙籤吞了，然後後半輩子都被自己瞎想出來的一大群鬼怪糾纏住。鬼扯，我跟你說，真是鬼扯淡！」史古基回答。

聽到這裡，鬼魂發出駭人的吼叫聲，它搖動鐵鍊，發出陰沉恐怖的聲響，嚇得史古基緊抓住椅子，以防自己昏倒跌下去。但是更可怕的事情還在後面，鬼魂好像是因為室內圍著頭巾太熱了，就把綁在頭上的方巾拆下來，結果下巴竟然掉到了胸前！

史古基跪倒在地上，雙手緊握在臉前。

「饒了我吧！可怕的鬼魂，你為什麼要來糾纏我？」他說。

「唯利是圖之輩，你相信我的存在了吧？」鬼魂
答道。

「我相信了，不得不信。但是，為什麼鬼魂會在
陽間走動？為什麼要來找我？」史古基說。

P. 46　「每個人的靈魂都要大江南北地四處行腳，在人
們之間行走。在世時，如果不能做到這一點，死後就註
定要再來遊蕩人間。哦，可憐的我！眼睜睜望著那些已
經無法分享的東西，那些東西原本都是在世時可以分享
並換來快樂的！」鬼魂回答道。

鬼魂又大吼一聲，搖動鐵鍊，搓著一雙鬼影幽幽的
手。

「你戴著腳鐐，」史古基用顫抖的聲音說，「這
是為什麼？」

「我戴的是我生前打造的鐵鍊，是我一環一環、
一吋一吋接起來的，我自願把它纏在腰間，自願戴
著。你覺得這個鐵鍊的樣子奇怪嗎？」鬼魂回答道。

史古基抖得更厲害了。

鬼魂緊接著又說，「你知道你為自己戴上的那條
結實的鐵鍊，有多重、多長嗎？在七年前的聖誕夜，你
的鐵鍊就已經和我這條一樣重、一樣長了。之後，你繼

續打造鐵鍊，如今已經是一條沉重無比的鐵鍊了！」

　　史古基看了一下四周的地板，想看看自己身邊否有五、六十噚[11]長的鐵鍊繞著，不過他什麼也沒看到。

P. 47　　「雅各，老雅各·馬里，」他哀求道，「再多說一點，說些安慰我的話，雅各！」

　　「該說的我都說了。」鬼魂回答，「耶柏尼澤·史古基，安慰的話來自別處，會由不同的使者來傳達給不同的人。我不能把我想說的告訴你，我只能再多說一點點。我不能休息，不能停留，不能在任何地方逗留。注意聽！生前，我的靈魂沒有走出過我們的帳房，我的靈魂一輩子沒有離開過我們那個狹小的兌幣窗口。如今，眼前等著我的，只有疲憊的旅程！」

　　史古基有個習慣，他在想事情的時候，會把兩手插在褲子的口袋裡。他思索著鬼魂說的話，兩手插在褲子的口袋裡，不過他仍跪在地上，眼睛也沒有抬起來。

　　「雅各，那你的動作一定很慢！」史古基恭恭敬敬、一臉正經地說道。

　　「很慢？」鬼魂重複道。

　　「死了七年，這段時間都在遊蕩？」史古基沉思

---

11 六十噚，約一百一十公尺。

乘著風，跟風一樣快！

道。

P. 49　「整整七年，沒有休息，也沒有平靜，不斷在懊悔中煎熬著。」鬼魂說。

　「你遊走的速度快嗎？」史古基問。

　「像乘著風的翅膀那樣快！」鬼魂回答。

　「那七年來，你應該已經走過不少的地方了吧。」史古基說。

P. 50　鬼魂聽到這裡，又發出一聲吼叫，把鐵鍊弄得噹啷作響，在這死寂的夜裡格外駭人，守衛要是聽到了，鐵定會告他妨害安寧。

　「哦！被囚禁、捆綁、銬上兩道鐵鐐的鬼魂，我寧可不要知道：塵世的善，在尚未圓滿之前，不死的鬼魂們幾百年來都要馬不停蹄地奔走，一直到永遠。我寧可不要知道：凡是具有基督精神的靈魂，都盡一己之力在行善，但是他們發現，不管是什麼善，能行的善太多了，而生命卻太短暫。我寧可不要知道：一個人的生命要是白白糟蹋浪費了，再多的悔恨也無法彌補！哦，我就是這樣，就是這樣啊！」鬼魂叫喊道。

P. 50　「可是，雅各，你生前的事業一直都做得很好！」史古基顫抖著聲音說道，他開始琢磨自己也會有同樣的下場。

「事業！人類才應該是我的事業，公眾福利才應該是我的事業！慷慨布施、仁慈憐憫、寬宏大量、心地善良，這些才應該是我的事業。在我應該做的事業中，我做的生意只是滄海一粟！」鬼魂嚷著，又開始搓揉雙手。

鬼魂伸長手臂，把鐵鍊舉起來，彷彿鐵鍊是它後悔莫及的緣由，然後又重重地把鐵鍊摔到地上。

P. 51　「年歲流逝，這個時節是我一年當中最難受的時候。為什麼以前我要低著頭走過熙嚷的人群，不抬頭看看那顆代表神聖的星星呢？那顆星星曾經引導東方三賢士到那卑微的住所，難道沒有窮苦人家能讓星光引導我去？」鬼魂說。

史古基很害怕鬼魂再繼續往下說，全身開始劇烈地顫慄起來了。

「聽我說！我的時間快用完了。」鬼魂叫道。

「我會聽，可是不要這樣嚇我！雅各，求求你，不要再說那些話！」史古基說道。

「我為什麼要以這副模樣出現在你面前，這我不能說。我坐在你身邊已經好些日子了，只是你看不到。」

這聽起來真不是什麼好事。史古基顫抖著，拭去眉毛上的汗珠。

「還會有三個幽靈來找你。」鬼魂繼續說道。

「我的贖罪一點也不輕鬆。今晚我來這裡就是要警告你，因為你還有機會和希望，可以避免和我一樣的命運。這是我特地為你爭取到的機會和希望呀，耶柏尼澤。」鬼魂緊接著又說。

P. 52

「你生前一直都是我的好友，謝了！」史古基說。

「還會有三個幽靈來找你。」鬼魂繼續說道。

史古基的臉垮了下來，不輸給鬼魂剛剛掉的下巴的樣子。

「雅各，難道這就是你剛才所說的機會和希望？」他顫抖著聲音問道。

「沒錯。」

「我……我想，我寧可不要。」史古基說。

「要是不讓它們來拜訪你，你就沒有希望避免步上我的後塵。明天鐘聲敲響一點鐘的時候，就等著第一位幽靈到訪吧。」鬼魂說道。

「雅各，不能請它們一起來，一次解決這件事情嗎？」史古基提議道。

「在隔天的同一時刻，等待第二個的到來。第三個又再隔一晚，十二點的鐘聲最後一聲敲完時會到來。不要期待再看見我。為了你自己好，不要忘了我們今晚所發生的事情！」

鬼魂說完，從桌子上拿起方巾，像先前一樣綁在頭上。史古基從牙齒相撞所發出的劇烈聲響，知道纏繞的方巾又將鬼魂的下巴給接上了。他壯起膽子，再度抬眼，看到這位鬼訪客直挺挺地站在面前，手臂上繞著一圈圈的鐵鍊。

P.54　　鬼魂從他面前往後退，每退一步，窗子就自動往上開一點，等鬼魂退到窗口時，窗子整個打開了。鬼魂招喚史古基走向前，史古基照做了。在相距不到兩步的距離時，馬里的鬼魂舉起手來，警告他不要再往前走，史古基便停了下來。

　　倒不是史古基對鬼魂言聽計從，而是他受到太多驚嚇了。鬼魂的手一舉起來，他就聽到窗外傳來嘈雜的聲音，那是斷斷續續的慟哭聲、悔恨聲、無法形容的悲慟和自責的哭訴聲。鬼魂傾聽了一會兒，然後加入這曲哀傷的輓歌中，接著飄出窗外，投入淒涼黑暗的夜空中。

　　史古基跟到窗邊，好奇心讓他不顧一切，他抬眼望向窗外。

　　夜空中擠滿了鬼魂，無止無休、匆匆忙忙地四處飄蕩著，並且一邊嗚咽著。它們和馬里的鬼魂一樣，身上繞著鐵鍊，有幾個被綁在一起（可能是犯了罪的官員），沒有一個是自由的。

P. 55　　有一些鬼魂在生前是史古基的舊識，一個穿著白色背心、腳踝上綁著巨大鐵製保險箱的老鬼魂，以前和史古基很熟，他哭得很悽慘，因為下方門口階梯上有一個抱著嬰兒的可憐婦女，他卻幫不了忙。顯然這些鬼魂的痛苦在於他們想出手為人們做些什麼事，卻永遠無能為力了。

　　史古基無法分辨到底是這些鬼魂走入了霧中，還是濃霧湧上淹沒了鬼魂。總之，鬼魂和鬼叫聲一起消失了，夜晚又恢復了原來的樣子，跟他剛剛走回家時一樣。

　　史古基關上窗戶，又去檢查鬼魂剛才走進來的那扇門。門仍是上了兩道鎖，跟他剛才親手鎖上的一樣，門閂也沒有人動過。他想開口說「鬼扯淡」，但一出聲音就又打住。可能是剛才受了太大的刺激，或是白天太操勞了，還是他撞鬼了，或是他和鬼魂的談話令人難受，又或者是時間太晚了，他直接走到床邊，衣服也沒脫，倒頭就睡了。

第二樂章

第一個幽靈

P. 56 　　史古基醒來時，四周一片漆黑，從床上望過去，房間裡，是透明的窗戶還是不透明的牆壁，難以分辨。他用雪貂似的眼睛，想在黑暗中看個清楚，這時候，附近教堂響起整點報時的鐘聲，他聆聽著現在是幾點鐘。

　　讓他驚駭的是，沉重的鐘聲從六點打到七點，從七點打到八點，有條不紊地一直打十二點，然後停住了，十二點！他上床的時候就已經過了凌晨兩點，這鐘壞了，一定是被冰柱卡住了！怎麼會是十二點呢！

　　他按了一下自己的打簧鐘，想要校正這荒謬的時鐘，結果打簧鐘的小發條急促打了十二下才停住。

　　「怎麼回事？不可能，我不可能睡了一整天，然後又睡到隔天半夜。也不可能是太陽出了問題，現在是中午十二點才對！」

P. 57　　一想到這裡，他嚇得滾下床來，摸黑走到窗口。他先用睡袍的袖子把霜氣擦掉，這樣才能看得到窗外，但是窗外一片朦朧。他只能分辨出外頭的霧還是很濃，非常寒冷，沒有行人穿梭的聲音。如果是白天已經將黑夜趕走，接管了世界，就會有人們熙來攘往的聲音。

　　還好的確不是白天，他鬆了一大口氣，否則白天如果都成了黑夜，日子就不知怎麼計算了，那麼「見此匯票第一聯三日後，應支付耶柏尼澤‧史古基先生或指定人」，諸如此類的東西就會變得和形同廢紙的美國債券一樣了。

　　史古基回到床上，想了又想，百思不得其解。他越想，就越糊塗；越是盡力不去想，就想得越多。馬里的鬼魂深深困擾著他，每次他冷靜推敲，想把它當作是一場夢時，心思卻像彈簧彈回原位那樣，反而又把問題從頭到尾地想了一遍，「那到底是不是在作夢？」

P. 58　　史古基就這樣躺著，直到傳來四十五分的鐘聲時，才突然想起鬼魂跟他說過，一點的鐘聲響起時，會有幽靈來訪。於是他決定睜著眼睛躺著，等待時間到來，況且要他現在再入睡，可比上天堂還難了，所以眼下這是最明智的作法了。

　　這一刻鐘好漫長，他不只一次覺得自己不小心打了

盹，錯過了時間。終於，鐘聲
傳進了他豎起的耳朵裡。

「叮，咚！」

「一刻鐘。」史古基數著
時間說道。

「叮，咚！」

「兩刻鐘。」史古基說。

「叮，咚！」

「三刻鐘。」史古基說。

「叮，咚！」

「整點鐘了，什麼事也沒
有！」史古基得意地說道。

整點的鐘聲還在響，低
沉、單調、空洞、淒涼的一點鐘響完之際，房間裡亮了
起來，床上的帷帳被掀了開來。

P. 59　　我跟你說，他床上的帷帳被一隻手給掀開了，不
是他腳邊的帷帳，也不是他背後的帷帳，而是正對著他
的臉孔的帷帳。他床上的帷帳被掀到一邊，史古基嚇了
一跳，他撐起半個身子，發現自己和那位拉開帷帳的幽
靈訪客正面對著面，就像現在你我一樣近，我站在幽靈
的位置，就在你的身邊。

幽靈的樣子很奇怪，像個小孩，但因為是幽靈，看起來更像老頭子，外形縮得比較小，比例上像小孩。它的頭髮披散在頸間，一直垂到背部，一頭老人的白髮，臉上卻無絲毫皺紋，皮膚泛著嬌嫩青春的紅光。一雙手臂長而有力，兩隻手也是，好像有超乎尋常的力氣。瘦小細長的雙腿和雙腳，也像上身的手臂一樣裸露著。

P.60　　它穿著一件潔白的長袍，腰間束著一條閃閃發光的腰帶，光芒耀眼。它的手裡拿著一根剛摘下來的綠色冬青樹枝，象徵著冬天，矛盾的是，它的衣服卻鑲著夏季的花朵。

然而最奇怪的是，它的頭冠發出明亮的光芒，照亮了周圍的一切。他的手臂夾著一頂帽子，無疑的，這帽子是絕佳的熄燈用具，要暗的時候就用帽子來遮住光線。

史古基又更仔細地瞧了瞧，發現還有更奇怪的：幽靈的腰帶會忽而這邊亮，忽而那邊亮，時而亮，時而暗。他的外形就隨著閃光變化著，一會兒變成只有一條胳膊，一會兒只有一條腿，一會兒有二十條腿，一會兒有一雙腿、沒有頭，一會兒有頭、沒有身體。那些消失不見的部分，融入漆黑的幽暗中，看不到一絲輪廓，然後怪異的樣子又會現回原形，清清楚楚的。

P. 61　　「先生，你就是預告說會來找我的那位幽靈？」史古基問道。

　　「就是我！」

　　幽靈的聲音輕輕柔柔的，很低沉，不像是在他身邊講出來的聲音，而像是從遠處傳來的。

　　「你是誰？要來做什麼？」史古基問。

　　「我是『往日聖誕幽靈』。」

　　「是古時候的聖誕節？」史古基注視著它矮小的身材問道。

　　「不是，是你個人過去的聖誕節。」

　　要是有人問起，史古基自己也不知怎麼的，就是很想看幽靈戴上帽子，於是他請求幽靈把頭上的光遮掉。

　　「什麼！你這麼快就要用世俗的手把我的光熄滅掉？就是你們這樣的人，這麼多年來，急於逼我把帽子壓在額頭上，難道這還不夠嗎？」幽靈喊道。

P. 63　　史古基恭恭敬敬地否認，說自己無意冒犯，也不知道自己一生中何曾逼過幽靈戴上帽子。接著，他大膽問了幽靈的來意。

　　「是為了你好！」幽靈說道。

「我是『往日聖誕幽靈』。」

史古基嘴裡說感謝，但心裡忍不住想，能讓他整晚睡個好覺，才是為他好。幽靈一定聽到了他的想法，因為幽靈立刻說：

　　「是為了感化你！注意了！」

　　幽靈說著，一邊伸出強壯的手，輕輕抓著他的手臂。

　　「起來！跟我走！」

　　史古基要是說這種天氣和時間都不適合在外散步，說床上很暖和，溫度計都掉到零下好幾度了，說他只有穿拖鞋、睡袍和睡帽，太單薄了，或是說他現在都感冒了，這樣跟它求情也是沒有用的。那隻手雖然柔軟得像女人的手，卻無法掙開。他起身，發現幽靈帶著他往窗口走去的時候，他抓住它的長袍懇求著。

P. 64　　「我只是個凡人，會掉下去的。」史古基抗議道。

　　「只要我的手碰你這裡，你就會飄得比現在還高！」幽靈說著，把手放在史古基的胸口上。

　　話一完，他們已經穿過牆壁，站在一條寬闊的鄉間馬路上了，路的兩旁都是田野。倫敦市已經完全消失不見，黑暗和濃霧也跟著一起消失，眼前是一個晴朗的寒冷冬日，地上覆蓋著白雪。

　　「天啊！我就是在這個地方長大的，我小時候就住在這裡！」史古基握緊雙手，看著四周的景色說。

　　幽靈溫和地看著他，溫柔的目光輕輕一閃而過，但史古基這個老人家還是感覺到了。他聞到空氣中的千百種味道，每種味道都讓他想起遺忘許久的無限思緒、希望、快樂和憂愁！

　　「你的嘴唇在顫抖！還有，你臉頰上的是什麼東西？」幽靈說。

　　史古基喃喃地說那是面皰，聲音哽咽，請求幽靈帶他去他想去的地方。

P. 65　　「你記得這條路嗎？」幽靈問道。

　　「記得！我蒙著眼睛都知道這條路怎麼走！」史古基熱切說道。

　　「那就奇怪了，這地方你都忘了那麼多年了！我們繼續走吧。」幽靈說。

　　他們沿著路行走，史古基認得每一扇門、每一根柱子、每一棵樹，接著，遠處出現一座小市鎮，那裡有一座橋、教堂和蜿蜒的河流。他們看到幾匹鬃毛蓬鬆的小馬正朝他們踏步跑過來，小孩子騎在馬背上，向坐在農夫駕駛的二輪馬車或貨車上的男孩們，大聲打著招呼。孩子們興高采烈，彼此叫喚著，寬闊的田野裡充滿了歡樂的音樂，連清新的微風都聽得笑了起來。

「這些都只是過去的塵影，他們感覺不到我們在這裡。」幽靈說。

快樂的孩子繼續前來。當孩子們走過來的時候，史古基都認出來了，而且喊得出每一個人的名字。為什麼他見到這些小孩會那麼興奮？孩子們走過去，他冷酷的眼睛怎會閃耀著光芒，一顆心會怦怦地跳呢？聽見孩子們在十字路口和岔路上道別，要各自回家，互相祝賀聖誕快樂時，他的心中為什麼會充滿喜悅呢？對史古基來說，聖誕節有什麼好快樂的？去他的聖誕快樂！聖誕節究竟給過他什麼好處呢？

P. 66 「學校並非空無一人，有一個孤單的孩子被朋友們拋棄了，一個人留在那裡。」幽靈說道。

史古基說他知道，便嗚咽啜泣了起來。

他們離開大馬路，走進一條熟悉的巷子裡，不久來到一棟暗紅磚的大房子，屋頂閣樓的上方有一座小小的風信雞，閣樓裡面掛了時鐘。房子很大，但是已經破舊。那些寬敞的辦公間很少使用，潮濕的牆壁長了苔蘚，窗戶也破了，門也壞了。畜舍裡，家禽咯咯叫，雄赳赳地走來走去，馬車房和棚屋裡長滿了雜草。

屋子裡面也是昔景不在，他們走進陰鬱的穿堂，看到許多房間的房門開著，房內冷清空盪，沒有什麼家具擺設。空氣中一股塵土味，淒淒涼涼一個地方，感覺這裡多的是要起早貪黑，少的是可以果腹的東西。

P. 68　　幽靈和史古基走過穿堂，來到房子的後門。門在他們面前打開，眼前是一間狹長、空盪、死氣沉沉的房間，裡面幾排簡陋的冷杉長凳和書桌，顯得愈發冷清。其中一張書桌前，坐著一個孤零零的男孩，他正挨著一簇微弱的爐火讀書。史古基在一張長凳上坐下來，流淚看著過去那個可憐的自己，他都忘了自己以前是這樣子的。

屋子裡的一點回音，牆壁嵌板後面老鼠的吱吱聲和扭打聲，房子後面的破落庭園裡，半結冰的水龍頭的滴水聲，蕭條的白楊樹上，光禿禿的枝椏間的窸窣聲，空蕩蕩的儲藏室的門，晃來晃去發出的開門聲，爐火裡的劈啪聲──任何的聲音，都能傳進史古基的心坎，令他感傷，淚流不停。

幽靈碰碰他的手臂，指著那個正專心看著書的年少自己。忽然，有一個人穿著異國服裝的男人，清清楚楚、真真實實地就站在窗外，腰帶上插著一把斧頭，牽著一隻馱著木柴的驢子。

P. 71　　「啊，那是阿里巴巴！」史古基興奮地喊道：

一張書桌前，坐著一個孤零零的男孩。

「是親愛、誠實的老阿里巴巴！沒錯，沒錯，我知道！有一年聖誕節，那個孤單的孩子被留在那裡的時候，他確實有來過。那次是第一次，跟這次完全一樣。可憐的孩子！還有弗倫坦因和他野蠻的弟弟奧森。他們走過去啦！還有，那個叫什麼的，他穿著內褲，在睡夢中被丟到大馬士革的城門前，你沒看見他嗎！還有那個蘇丹馬車伕，被妖怪倒吊著，他現在是頭下腳上！我很高興他受到處罰，那是自作自受，他憑什麼娶公主？」

史古基在倫敦市的商界朋友，要是聽到他用這麼一種又哭又笑的聲音，一本正經地談論這些事情，再看到他激動興奮的表情，一定會吃個大驚，真的！

「有隻鸚鵡！綠色的身體，黃色的尾巴，頭頂上長著一個像萵苣的東西，牠在那裡！可憐的魯賓遜，魯賓遜繞著荒島航行一圈，等他回到家裡，鸚鵡這麼對他叫著，『可憐的魯賓遜，你到哪裡去了，魯賓遜？』魯賓遜以為自己在作夢，但那不是作夢，你知道的，那是鸚鵡在叫他。還有那個星期五，他拼命逃向小海灣！快啊！加油！加油！」史古基又喊了起來。

P. 72　　接著，他一反常態，情緒突然一變，可憐起以前的自己，說道：「可憐的孩子！」然後又哭了起來。

「我希望……」史古基用袖子擦乾眼淚，然後把手伸進口袋，向四周望了望，喃喃自語道：「可是現在已經太遲了。」

「怎麼了？」幽靈問。

「沒什麼，沒什麼。只是想起昨天晚上，有個小男孩在我的門口唱聖誕歌，我應該給他一點什麼才對。就這樣！」史古基說。

幽靈親切地笑了笑，把手一揮，說道：「我們來看看另一個聖誕節！」

才說完，史古基小時候的身形就變大了，房間也變得暗一些、髒一些。牆壁的嵌版萎縮，窗戶破裂，天花板的灰泥碎片掉落，露出了木板條。眼前一切是怎麼變化出來的，史古基跟你一樣不明白。他只知道是這個樣子沒錯，當時一切確實是這樣，男孩們都快快樂樂回家過節了，他又孤孤單單一個人留了下來。

他這次不是在看書，而是頹喪地走來走去。史古基看著幽靈，一臉悲傷地搖著頭，焦急地朝著門口望去。

P. 73　　門打開了，一個比男孩小很多的小女孩飛快地跑進來，張開雙臂抱住男孩的脖子，不停地親吻他，喊著「親愛、親愛的哥哥」。

「親愛的哥哥，我是來接你回家的。接你回家，回家，回家！」小女孩拍著小手，彎著腰笑道。

「回家嗎，小芳？」男孩答道。

「對！」女孩歡天喜地地說：「回家，以後不用回來了。回家，永永遠遠住在家裡。爸爸比以前好很多，現在家裡就像天堂一樣！有一天晚上，我正要上床睡覺，爸爸很溫和地跟我說話，我沒有害怕，就又大膽地問說可不可以讓你回家。他說可以，說你也該回家了，還要我坐馬車來接你。你就要變成大人了！」女孩睜大了眼睛說：「你再也不用回來這裡了。不過，我們要先一起度過一個全世界最快樂的聖誕假期。」

「你已經像大人了，小芳！」男孩喊道。

她拍著手笑著，想摸哥哥的頭，但是個子太小，搆不著。她又笑了起來，踮著腳尖抱住哥哥，然後孩子氣地急著把他拖到門邊，哥哥也恭敬不如從命地跟著走。

P.74　　一陣可怕的叫喊聲在穿堂裡響了起來，「來呀！把史古基少爺的箱子搬下來！」這時，校長出現在穿堂裡，嚴厲而高傲地瞪著史古基少爺，然後跟他握了握手，讓他怕得要命。

之後，校長帶他和妹妹來到會客室，裡面陰冷得像古井，牆壁上掛著的地圖和窗台上的星象儀、地球儀，都凍得像上了一層蠟。校長拿出一瓶口味怪怪的淡

他把點心分給兩個小客人，一人一份。

葡萄酒、一塊口味濃得很怪的蛋糕，然後把點心分給這兩個年輕人。同時，他派了一個瘦弱的僕人，送一杯喝的給馬車伕。馬車伕回覆說，他感謝校長，不過，如果那是他以前喝過的那種酒，那就心領了。

這時候，史古基少爺的行李已經裝上馬車頂，兩個孩子欣然地向校長道別。他們坐進馬車，興高采烈地沿著校園彎道驅車揚長而去，飛馳的車輪輾過常青樹的暗色葉子，震落了葉面上的白霜和雪花，宛如四處飛濺的浪花。

P. 77 「她一直很嬌弱，吹口氣就可以把她吹倒，但是她心胸寬大！」幽靈說。

「她是心胸寬大，你說得沒錯。幽靈，我不否認，不然天理不容！」史古基說道。

「她過世時已經結婚了，我記得她有小孩。」幽靈說道。

「一個小孩。」史古基回答道。

「對，就是你的外甥！」幽靈說。

史古基心裡似乎有些難受，簡短說道：「對。」

他們才剛離開學校，轉眼就來到城市裡熱鬧的大街上。路上行人的朦朧身影來來往往，貨車和馬車的模糊影子爭相搶道，現在出現了一個真實存在的城市所該有的嘈雜和喧囂。從那些商店的布置看來，顯然這裡也在過聖誕節。不過現在是晚上了，街道上的燈都點亮了。

幽靈停在一家商店門前，問史古基知不知道這家店。

「何止知道！我就在這裡當學徒！」史古基說。

他們走進店裡，一個戴著威爾斯假髮的老紳士，坐在一張很高的桌子後面，他要是再高個兩吋，頭就會碰到天花板了。史古基一看見他，激動地叫嚷起來：

P. 78

「啊，是老費茲威格！哎呀，他又活過來了！」

老費茲威格把筆放下，抬頭看看時鐘，時鐘指著七點。他搓了搓手，整理一下身上那件寬大的背心，滿懷笑容，從頭到腳渾身都是笑意，然後用圓潤響亮、厚實快活的愉快聲音喊道：

「喲荷，快來呀！耶柏尼澤！迪克！」

當年的小史古基，現在已經是一位年輕人了，他輕快地跑進來，另一個學徒跟在身邊。

「沒錯，是迪克‧威爾金！天啊，沒錯，他就在那裡！他以前跟我很要好，是迪克，可憐的迪克！天哪！」史古基對幽靈說道。

「喲荷，孩子們！今天晚上就做到這裡了，是聖誕夜呢，迪克。是聖誕節啊，耶柏尼澤！上門板吧，越快越好！」老費茲威格兩手用力一拍喊道。

你一定不相信這兩個傢伙的動作有多快！他們拿著門板衝到街上——一、二、三——門板就裝上去了——四、五、六——門閂就拴上了——七、八、九——你還來不及數到十二，他們就已經跑回來了，像賽馬一樣喘著氣。

P. 80　「嘿嘿，喝！把東西挪開，孩子們！把地方讓出來！嘿嘿，喝，迪克！嘖嘖，耶柏尼澤！」老費茲威格喊道，一邊優美靈活地從高桌後面跳下來。

把東西搬走！在老費茲威格的監督下，他們沒有不願搬或是搬不動的東西。東西一下子就移開堆在一旁，好像從此就要從大家的生活中消失似的。地板打掃清洗過了，燈蕊修剪過了，爐火堆滿了炭。商店搖身一變成為你在冬夜裡最想看到的舒適溫暖、乾爽明亮的舞廳。

一位小提琴師帶著樂譜走進來，他爬到高桌上，把那裡當作演奏台，調出來的音像五十個人胃絞痛的呻吟聲。費茲威格夫人來了，臉上笑容可掬。三位討喜可愛的費茲威格小姐來了，後面跟著六個為她們心碎的年輕追求者。這家店聘僱的年輕男女都來了。女僕也帶著當麵包師傅的表哥進來了。廚師帶著她哥哥那位送牛

270

「唷荷，孩子們！今天晚上就做到這裡了，是聖誕夜呢！」

奶的朋友一起來。住在對面的男孩進來了，大家都猜測，他的主人給他的食物量不夠他吃，男孩這時正想辦法躲在隔壁家的女孩身後，這位女孩的耳朵顯然剛被女主人揪過。

P. 82　　全部的人都到齊了，一個接著一個，有的害羞，有的大膽，有的得體，有的笨拙，有的推來拉去，總之大家都來了。他們開始跳舞，一下子就有二十對下去跳舞，手搭手轉了半個圓圈，又從另一個方向轉回來，跳到中間又跳回來，轉啊轉，一對對熱情的舞者跳出各式各樣的舞步。帶頭的舞者老是搞錯位置，後面接棒帶頭的一走到那裡，就重新開始，結果大家都變成帶頭的，後面沒有人接應了。

　　老費茲威格一見狀，就拍手停止跳舞，喊道：「跳得好啊！」臉龐熱烘烘的小提琴師，趁機灌下一杯為他準備好的黑啤酒。但他不屑休息，儘管沒有半個人在跳舞了，仍立刻演奏起來，彷彿剛才的樂師已經累到讓人用門板抬回家，他是剛接手的樂師，不打敗之前的樂師，他就不罷手。

　　大家又跳了幾支舞，玩了幾輪「沒收東西」的罰物遊戲，又再跳了幾支舞。席上有蛋糕、尼格斯熱甜酒、一大塊冷的烤牛肉和水煮牛肉、碎肉餅和一大堆啤

他不屑休息，
立刻又演奏起來。

酒。今晚的壓軸，排在吃烤牛肉和水煮牛肉之後。當小
提琴師（注意！他是那麼機伶，不用別人交代，就能把
事情做得令人喜出望外）奏起那首《羅吉‧克弗利爵
士》的舞曲時，老費茲威格和太太走出來，帶頭跳這
支舞，這可不是一件輕鬆的事，跟在他們後面跳的有
二十三、四對之多，這些人是不能唬弄的，他們跳舞比
走路還內行。

P. 83　　不過，就算人數再來個兩倍、四倍，老費茲威格

老費茲威格和太太走出來，帶頭跳這支舞。

先生和太太也都應付得來。說到太太，她各方面都足以和先生匹配，這樣說如果還不夠恭維，要是還有更高的讚嘆，我會欣然採用。老費茲威格的小腿彷彿會發出亮光，像月光般照亮每一個舞步，你根本猜不到他下一刻會跳出什麼樣的舞步。

老費茲威格和太太跳完整首曲子，他們一個前進、一個後退，拉著對方的手，一個鞠躬、一個屈膝回禮，在隊伍裡交叉穿梭，高舉交握的手，讓隊伍從底下穿過去，再回到原位。老費茲威格跳到半空中，雙腿一剪，巧妙地像是用兩條腿在眨眼睛，然後落地，雙腳站定，一晃也不晃。

P. 85　　當鐘敲響十一點，家庭舞會結束了。費茲威格夫婦分別站在門的兩旁，跟每個走出去的男女客人一一握手，祝賀他們聖誕快樂。等大家都走了，只剩那兩個學徒，他們也同樣跟他們握手，祝福他們聖誕快樂。這時，歡樂的聲音才止息下來，留下兩位年輕人，他們的床就在後間店舖的櫃檯下。

在這整場舞會的時間裡，史古基像是失了魂。他的心思沉浸在那些畫面裡，想著過去的自己。眼前的每一件事情都確實發生過，他都記得，也都很投入過，領受過那莫名的激動。一直到年輕時的自己和迪克把容光

煥發的臉龐轉開，史古基這才想到了幽靈，他發現幽靈
正盯著他看，頭頂上的光芒很明亮。

「一點小事，就讓這些愚蠢的傢伙這麼感恩。」
幽靈說道。

「小事！」史古基重複道。

幽靈示意他注意聽那兩個學徒的談話，他們正滿
心感激地稱讚著費茲威格。等史古基聽完，幽靈說：

P. 87 「怎麼！難道不是嗎？他不過是花了凡間的幾個
錢，三、四鎊吧，有多到值得你們這麼讚嘆嗎？」

「話不能這麼說。」史古基說，幽靈的話讓他激
動起來，說話不自覺地回到以前的樣子，不像他後來那
樣。「話不能這麼說啊，幽靈。他有辦法讓我們快樂或
不快樂，讓我們的工作可輕鬆、可繁重，可以有趣，也
可以是苦哈哈的。就算只是說話或神情這樣微不足道
的、不值一文錢的東西，那又怎麼樣？他帶給我們的快
樂，像是花一大筆錢才能換來的。」

他發現幽靈在看他，便打住了。

「怎麼啦？」幽靈問道。

「沒什麼。」史古基答道。

「一定有什麼事吧？」幽靈追問道。

「沒有，就是沒有。」」史古基說：「我只是巴

不得現在就跟我的文書員說句話罷了！就這樣。」

　　在他說出這個願望之際，那個年輕的他把燈關小，史古基和幽靈又並肩站在屋外了。

　　「我的時間快到了，快點！」幽靈說道。

　　這句話並不是對史古基或是任何眼前的人說的，話一說完，場景就變了。史古基看見再年長些的自己，那是個正值壯年的男人，臉上還沒有老年時那些嚴酷深鑿的皺紋，但是已經出現了汲於利益的樣子了。他帶著利欲熏心、汲汲營營的眼神，顯示欲念已經在心裡紮了根，逐漸長大的樹將會投下陰影。

P. 88　　這時他並非單獨一人，身邊坐著一位穿著喪服的美麗少婦，眼中含著淚水，淚水在「往日聖誕幽靈」散發出的光芒下閃耀著。

　　「這沒什麼關係，對你沒有什麼差別。另一個寵兒已經取代了我，它在以後的日子裡可以安慰你、鼓舞你，就像我以前那樣，我也沒有什麼理由可以難過的了。」她輕柔地說道。

　　「什麼寵兒取代了你？」他問。

　　「金子打造出來的寵兒。」

　　「人世間的交易就是這麼公平！人生最難受的，是貧窮；最被譴責的，卻是追求財富！」他說。

「你太畏懼這個世界了，你所有的希望只剩下一個，不讓勢利之徒有機會蔑視你。我看著你崇高的抱負一個個消逝，最後只剩下賺錢的欲望占據了你，我看到的不就是這樣嗎？」她溫和地答道。

P. 89 「那又怎樣？就算我現在變得聰明多了，又怎樣？我對你的心沒有變呀！」他反駁道。

她搖搖頭。

「我有變嗎？」

「我們的誓約已經不再了，那時我們沒有錢，可是很知足，只希望靠著辛勤工作，早日改善經濟。但是，你變了。你當初不是這樣的人。」

「我那時候還年輕。」他不耐煩地說。

「你自己也知道，你不再是以前的你了，而我還是以前的我。以前，我們兩人同心時，幸福近在眼前；現在我們不同心了，只留下悲悽。我就不說我有多麼憂心了。總之我想通了，我就放你走吧。」她說。

「我有要你放我走嗎？」

「你嘴巴上是沒說過。」

「那我是怎樣了？」

「你的個性變了，你的心變了，你過不一樣的生活了，只有那個願望才是你最大的目標。在你眼中，我的愛不再像以前那樣是最珍貴的。如果我們沒有過這一段感情，告訴我，」女子柔和卻堅定地看著他：「現在的你還會想追求我嗎？會想贏得我的心嗎？不會的！」

P. 90 這個推測並沒有誣賴人，他難以否認，不過他最後不情願地說了一句：「是你覺得不會。」

「但願我可以不這麼想，天知道。當我看出這個真相的時候，已經無法挽回了。假設你現在、未來、過去都是單身，我還能相信你會選擇娶一個沒有嫁妝的女孩嗎？就算你和她很親密，你還是會用金錢來衡量一切。如果，你因為一念之差，違背了你最高的準則而選擇娶了她，隨後一定會懊悔，這我會不清楚嗎？我很清楚的，所以我讓你走。我是真心的，畢竟我以前是你愛的人。」她答道。

他想開口說話，但是她把頭轉開繼續說道：

「念及我們的過去，我想你或許也會痛苦，但是痛苦很快就會過去，你會開心地忘記過去，當它不過是一場沒有用的空夢，自己正好可以夢醒了。祝你自己選擇的人生能幸福快樂！」

P. 93 她離開他，兩人就此分手了。

「幽靈！不要再給我看什麼了！帶我回家吧，你

祝你在自己選擇的人生中過得愉快！

為什麼要這麼樂於折磨我？」史古基說。

「再看一幕就好了！」幽靈說道。

「不要了！不要了，我不想看。不要再給我看了！」史古基叫嚷道。

但是無情的幽靈用兩隻手臂挾住他，要他看下一幕。

他們來到另一個場景和地點：一間房間，不是很大、很漂亮，但是很舒適。冬天的爐火旁，坐著一個美麗的年輕女孩，和剛剛那個女子很像，史古基以為是剛剛那一幕，直到看到她坐在女兒的對面，才發現她現在是一個美麗的少婦了。房間裡鬧哄哄的，有好幾個小孩，激動的史古基數不出來有幾個小孩。他們不像詩中那群有名氣的牛[1]，不是四十個小孩乖得像只有一個小孩那樣，而是每個小孩都吵得像有四十個小孩那麼多。

P. 94　屋子裡鬧翻天了，但好像沒有人在意，母女倆反倒開懷大笑，玩得很開心。女孩隨後也加入混戰，遭到那幫小土匪無情的掠奪。

1　指英國浪漫主義詩人華茲渥斯（William Wordsworth）的詩《寫於三月》（*Written in March*），其中一句寫道：「牛群埋頭吃草，四十隻牛每隻看起來都一樣。」（The cattle are grazing, Their heads never raising; There are forty feeding like one!）

一群興沖沖、鬧哄哄的孩子

　　只要能跟他們一起玩，你要什麼我都給你。而且我才不會像他們那麼粗魯！就算拿全世界的財富來換，我也不會弄亂她的辮子，還把它扯散。我說什麼也不會把她可愛的小鞋子硬脫下來。

　　天啊！那些放肆的小鬼，竟然抓著她的腰取樂，這種事我怎樣也做不出來。我的手要是敢放在她的腰上，手就會受到懲罰，再也別想伸直了。

　　不過，我承認真想碰觸她的小嘴，問她一些問題，好讓她能張開嘴唇。我想看著她垂眸上的睫毛，而且我不會臉紅。我也想讓她放下一頭波浪鬈髮，她的每一吋髮絲都是無價的紀念品。總之，我承認我想像孩子那樣可以放肆一下，但又能像個大人，知道這有多麼難能可貴。

P. 95　　這時傳來了敲門聲，孩子一陣爭先恐後，鬧哄哄地立刻簇擁著她走到門口，她帶著笑意，衣裳有些凌亂，剛好迎接上進門的父親。父親身旁跟著一個人，捧著好多聖誕節的玩具和禮物，接著一陣叫嚷與爭奪，送貨人慘遭攻擊，毫無招架之力！他們把椅子當梯子，爬到他身上，把手伸到他的袋子裡，搶走咖啡色的包裹！小鬼頭緊緊抓著他的頭巾，抱著他的脖子，拳頭打在他的背上，腳踢在他的腿上，無比熱情！在一陣陣驚喜的叫喊聲中，他們把每個包裹都拿到手了！

　　突然有人吃驚地說，小嬰兒把洋娃娃的煎鍋放進自己的嘴巴，有可能也把黏在木盤上的假火雞吞下去了！發現這是一場虛驚時，大伙鬆了好大一口氣！真是歡樂、感恩，無比欣喜啊！當孩子們帶著興奮的情緒走出客廳、上樓睡覺，才逐漸平靜了下來。

P. 97　　這時，史古基的眼睛盯著更緊了，屋子的男主人和妻女坐在壁爐邊，女兒撒嬌地靠在他身上。史古基想著，自己原本也會有這樣一個前途無量的優雅女孩叫他爸爸，為他人生的寒冬帶來春天，想著想著，視線模糊了起來。

　　「貝麗，我今天下午看到了你的一位老朋友。」丈夫把頭轉向妻子，微笑地說。

　　「誰啊？」

　　「你猜！」

　　「我怎麼猜得到！哎，不知道！」她馬上又加上一句，也笑了起來，「是史古基先生？」

　　「正是史古基先生。我路過他公司的窗口，那時他們還沒有下班，屋裡點了根蠟燭，我忍不住看了他一下。聽說他的合夥人病得差不多了，他就一個人坐在那裡。我想他在這個世上一定很孤單。」

那個人抱著許多聖誕節的玩具和禮物

「幽靈！帶我離開這個地方吧。」史古基聲音哽咽。

「我告訴過你，這是過去的塵影，都是發生過的事，別怪我。」幽靈說道。

「帶我離開！我受不了！」史古基喊道。

他回頭看幽靈，幽靈望著他，奇怪的是，幽靈今晚帶他見過的所有臉，這時爭相交映在幽靈臉上。

「走開！帶我回去，不要再來糾纏我！」

在和幽靈拉扯中（姑且說是拉扯吧，雖然幽靈沒有反抗，對手也動不了它什麼），史古基看見幽靈頭上的光芒愈來愈高、愈來愈亮。他突然靈光乍現，想到了自己為什麼會被控制，便一把抓起帽子，朝到幽靈的頭上叩下去。

帽子下面的幽靈縮了下去，整個被帽子蓋住。史古基使勁把帽子往下壓，但是無法遮住光芒，帽子下的光芒源源不絕地射出來，照在地上。

史古基感覺累壞了，抵不過睡意，下一刻就回到了自己的房間。他又按了一下帽子，然後鬆開手，腳步踉蹌，簡直來不及爬上床，就睡翻過去了。

第三樂章

第二個幽靈

P. 100 　　史古基在自己震天嘎響的鼾聲中醒來，坐在床上理了理思緒。不容旁人提醒他也知道一點的報時又要響起了。他覺得自己會在這個緊要關頭醒來，就是為了和雅各·馬里安排的第二個幽靈見面，只是不知道幽靈會從哪邊掀開他的床帳，一想到這裡就渾身發冷，很不舒服。他乾脆親手把每邊床帳全給掀開，然後躺下來緊盯床的四周。他希望幽靈一現身就能正面相迎，以免受驚嚇、緊張兮兮的。

P. 102 　　有些人總是一派輕鬆，吹噓自己很機靈、經驗老道，說不論什麼事情，舉凡從丟擲銅板到殺人，都難不倒他。當然啦，在丟擲銅板和殺人這兩個極端之間，什麼事都有。雖然史古基犯不著去做這麼困難的事，不過我倒是提醒一下，他可是做足了準備，不管出現什麼奇奇怪怪的東西，像是小嬰兒還是大犀牛，可都嚇不了他。

時鐘敲響一點鐘

這一刻，他準備就緒去面對任何東西的出現，卻沒料到什麼東西都沒出現。當一點的鐘聲敲完，卻不見任何動靜時，他反而一陣哆嗦。五分鐘、十分鐘、十五分鐘過去，還是沒有任何動靜。

他躺在床上，一片紅光投射在他身上，鐘聲響起後就一直朝他照著。他不知道紅光為何而來，這比十二個鬼魂還更令人警覺。片刻間，他擔心身體會在毫無防備下自燃起來，成一了一樁被人取笑的奇聞趣事。

P. 103 不過最後他終於想到（要是你我當下早就會想到了，只有非當局者才會清楚明白該怎麼做，也會毫不遲疑去做）這裝神弄鬼的亮光來源和秘密可能就在隔壁房。他追溯亮光源，發現光似乎是從那邊出來的沒錯。這想法占據了心頭，他輕手輕腳地爬下床，穿上拖鞋走到門口。

史古基的手一放在門鎖上，就聽到一個奇怪的聲音呼喚著他的名字，要他進去，他便進了房間。

不用質疑那確實是他自己的房間沒錯，但那房間卻有了驚人的變化。牆壁天花板掛滿了綠葉，像一片小樹林。林中處處都有鮮艷的莓果閃耀著光彩。冬青、檞寄生和常春藤鮮嫩樹葉反射著亮光，宛若散落的一面面小鏡子。

壁爐的火熊熊地燃燒著，朝煙囪竄起。不管住在這裡的是馬里還是史古基，過了無數寒冬，一向沉悶得像化石的壁爐，還是頭一次出現這番景象。

P. 104　地板像國王的寶座堆滿了各色東西，火雞、鵝、野味、雞鴨、醃豬肉、大塊肉、乳豬、一串串香腸、碎肉派、葡萄乾布丁、一桶桶的牡蠣、熱呼呼的栗子、鮮紅的蘋果、多汁的柳澄、甘甜的梨子、主顯節的大蛋糕，還有很多用碗盛著的熱騰騰調酒，這些美食蒸騰的香氣，弄得房間都模糊了。

一個快樂巨人舒舒服服地坐著沙發上，看起來很耀眼。他高舉一根形狀就像「豐饒號角」的燃燒火把，史古基在門口探頭張望時，火光正好照亮了他。

「進來！老兄，進來！好好過來認識認識我！」幽靈大聲喊道。

史古基膽怯地走進去，在幽靈面前垂低著頭。他不再是那個冥頑不靈的史古基了，雖然幽靈眼神明亮仁慈，但是他仍不想直視。

「我是『今日聖誕幽靈』，抬頭看著我！」幽靈說道。

「我是『今日聖誕幽靈』，抬頭看著我！」幽靈說道。

P.106　　史古基恭敬地照做了。幽靈穿著樣式簡單、滾著白毛邊的深綠色長袍或披風之類的。衣服鬆垮垮地披在身上，露出寬闊的胸膛，像是不屑受到任何東西的保護或遮掩。袍子下擺寬大的衣摺下，露出一雙赤腳。頭上沒有東西，只戴了冬青樹枝編織成的花冠，上面是閃閃發亮的冰柱。深褐色的長鬈髮自然地披落，呼應著親切的臉龐、閃爍的眼睛、張開的手、愉快的聲音、不拘的舉止和快樂的神情。幽靈的腰間掛著一把古劍鞘，但是沒有寶劍，只見老舊的劍鞘鏽跡斑斑。

「你沒見過像我這樣的人吧！」幽靈大聲說道。

「沒有。」史古基開口回答。

「也沒有和我家族年輕一輩的出去過？因為我還年輕，所以我是指近幾年才出生的哥哥們。」幽靈又問。

「應該沒有，我想是沒有跟它們出去過。你有很多哥哥嗎，幽靈？」史古基說。

P.108　　「一千八百多個。」幽靈說。

「這麼大一個家庭，負擔一定很重！」史古基喃喃自語道。

今日聖誕幽靈站了起來。

「幽靈，你要帶我去哪裡都可以！我昨晚被帶走，得到了教訓，現在學乖了。今天晚上，你想讓我知道什麼，就請便吧。」史古基順從地說道。

「拉著我的長袍！」

史古基照辦，緊緊抓著長袍。

冬青、槲寄生、紅莓果、常春藤、火雞、鵝肉、野味、雞鴨、醃肉、大塊肉、乳豬、香腸、牡蠣、派、布丁、水果和調酒，一眨眼功夫都不見了。房間、爐火、艷紅的火光和夜色也都消失了，此刻他們站在聖誕節早上的倫敦街道上，天氣嚴寒，人們在住家前的人行道和屋頂上鏟雪，傳出粗糙、輕快但並不難聽的樂音。積雪從屋頂砸落到下方街道上，像小小的人造暴風雪，男孩子們看得全樂瘋了。

房子的前門看起來黑漆漆，窗戶更黑，和屋頂平滑的白雪及地上稍髒的積雪形成對比。地上積的雪被貨車和馬車沉重的車輪輾過，留下深深的輪溝，街道路口處，輪溝相互交錯輾過千百回，形成錯綜複雜的水渠，在濃濁的黃泥漿和冰水的覆蓋下，變得難以辨識。

P.109　　天色陰暗，小街上彌漫著半凍結的濛濛濃霧。霧裡較重的煤煙灰塵，一陣陣飄散沉落下來，彷彿大英帝國境內所有的煙囪約好了要同時生火，盡情燒個痛快。這種天氣和這個城市，雖然沒有什麼特別的喜

這種天氣和這個城市，雖然沒有什麼特別的喜事，
卻也洋溢著歡樂的氣氛。

事，倒也洋溢著歡樂的氣氛，這就是夏天清新的空氣和明亮的太陽所做不到的事了。

屋頂上鏟雪的人們歡喜快活，他們隔著屋頂的矮牆彼此叫喚，不時互丟雪球鬧著玩。這比互相打嘴砲好多了，雪球打中了就哈哈大笑，打歪了也笑開懷。

P. 111 雞鴨店的門半掩著，水果店擺滿了鮮豔欲滴的水果。大圓竹簍裡裝滿栗子，彷如身穿背心的快活老紳士，懶洋洋地靠門邊，胖得都快中風的身軀就要滾到街上。

圓滾滾的西班牙紅洋蔥，長得像西班牙修士那樣胖呼呼的，在架子上賊頭賊腦地對著路過的女孩眨眼睛，又道貌岸然地瞄著掛在上面的槲寄生。梨子和蘋果高高地堆成一座座輝煌的金字塔，店家把一串串葡萄掛在最惹人注目的鉤子上，路人可以免費看得口水直流。

一堆堆長著絨毛的褐色榛子，散發的香氣讓人想起了古人在林中漫步，愉快地走在深及腳踝的枯葉上的光景。還有黑黑的扁胖烤諾福克蘋果，結實多汁，和柳橙、檸檬的黃色形成對比，苦苦懇請著人們把它們裝進紙袋裡帶回家，晚餐後可以大口享用。

P. 112 在這些上好的水果中，擺著一個魚缸，裡面養著金色和銀色的魚，雖然牠們是不怎麼聰明的冷血動物，但似乎也嗅出今天有什麼大事在進行著，在小小的世界裡些許興奮地一圈圈地緩緩游動著。

雜貨店！哦，還有雜貨店！差不多打烊了，有一兩片門板已放下去，但是瞧瞧門隙中的景象吧，裡頭好不熱鬧！有秤敲落在櫃檯的悅耳聲，包貨用的麻繩快速地轉動離開滾軸。茶葉罐和咖啡罐拿上拿下，嘎嘎作響，像在玩雜耍球似的。茶和咖啡的香氣混在一起，聞起來沁入心脾。店裡還有許多稀有的葡萄乾，白皙皙的杏仁，肉桂枝又直又長，各類香料香氣濃郁，裹著糖衣的醃漬蜜餞，連最不感興趣的路人看了也都頭暈反胃了。

無花果多汁多肉，精美的盒子裝著泛著嫣紅的微酸法國李子，在聖誕節的包裝下，什麼看起來都很可口。在這充滿期待的日子裡，顧客來往匆匆，人們在店門口彼此撞個滿懷，藤籃被粗魯地撞來撞去，再不然就是有人買了東西卻忘了拿，又急忙返回櫃檯拿。狀況層出不窮，但是沒人引以為意。雜貨老闆和夥計們親切熱情，圍裙用擦得發亮的心型別針別在背後，彷彿那是他們的真心似的，就算袒露在外任人檢視，或是聖誕寒鴉要來啄食也無妨。

P. 113　不久，教堂尖塔的鐘聲響起，召喚善良人們前往教堂和禮拜堂。大家穿上最好的衣服，笑容滿面，成群結隊地湧上街道。這時，也有很多人從街道巷弄走出來，拿著晚餐到麵包店[1]。看著這些窮人，幽靈很感興趣，它和史古基並肩站在麵包店門口，當窮人經過他們走進店裡，它就打開他們手上的食物蓋子，灑下一些火把上的香[2]。

P. 114 這支火把可不尋常，有一兩次拿著晚餐的人互相推擠，發生爭執，幽靈就從火把滴幾滴水在他們的身上，人們的火氣立刻消下來，直說在聖誕節這天吵架，真是丟臉。的確！這可是上帝眷顧的日子！

不久，鐘聲停止，麵包店也關門了。可喜的是，每家麵包店的烤爐上面，從潮濕融化的痕跡來看，可以得知食物都烘焙過了。街道上霧氣騰騰，彷彿街道的石板也在煮著東西。

「你從火把上灑下來的東西，有什麼特殊的味道嗎？」史古基問。

「有，是我獨家配方的味道。」

「今天所有的晚餐，你都會灑？」史古基問。

「人們好心供養的食物都會灑，尤其是供養給窮

---

1 當時的法令規定，在星期日和聖誕節，麵包店不能營業，所以窮人家要自己拿食材去麵包店烘焙，才有熟食可以吃。
2 在《聖經》裡，東方三賢士帶來三項禮物，其中一項就是乳香。

人的食物。」

「為什麼給窮人的食物特別會灑？」史古基問。

「因為窮人最需要。」

「幽靈，」史古基想了一會後說道：「在我們周圍各種世界的眾生之中，我不懂為什麼你就要妨礙這些人享受單純快樂的機會。」

P. 115 「我！」幽靈叫了起來。

「每隔七天，你就剝奪他們好好吃一頓飯的機會，對吧？他們往往只有在那一天才能吃到像樣的一餐。」史古基說道。

「我？」幽靈喊道。

「是你要這些麵包店星期日打烊的，不是嗎？結果就是造成現在這個樣子。」史古基說。

「是我幹的嗎？」幽靈大聲嚷道。

「我要是說錯了，請原諒。但這是以你的名義進行的，至少是以你家族的名義來做的[3]。」史古基說道。

「在你們的世界裡，有人自稱認識我們，打著我們的名義，做出狂熱、傲慢、惡意、憎恨、嫉妒、偏執、

3　星期日是基督教的安息日，所以規定麵包店不能營業。又因為這位幽靈是「今日聖誕幽靈」，所以史古基假設幽靈是上帝派來的。

自私的勾當，我們所有的親戚朋友根本不認識他們，也不知道他們的存在。請記住，他們自己做的事，要自己承擔，不要算到我們的頭上。」幽靈回答。

P. 116 史古基應允了幽靈。像先前一樣，他們繼續前進，人們看不到他們，這時他們來到了市郊。幽靈有一個神奇的能力（在麵包店門口的時候，史古基就注意到了），幽靈體型高大，卻能輕易地出入任何地方，就算站在低矮的屋頂下，也能像站在大廳裡那樣，流露出神界人物的高貴優雅。

這位善心幽靈是想賣弄自己出入自如的能力嗎？還是只是出於仁慈、慷慨、誠懇的本性，和對窮人的憐憫之心，所以幽靈直接來到了史古基的文書員家裡。史古基抓著幽靈的長袍，跟著一起走。來到門口時，幽靈停住腳步，笑了笑，拿著火把對著鮑伯·克瑞奇的家灑香賜福。你想想看吧！鮑伯一星期賺十五個「先令」⁴，每個星期六放進口袋裡的只有十五個和自己同名的東西，然而，「今日聖誕幽靈」卻來賜福給這個只有四個房間的屋子！

4　英文作「Bob」，Bob是人名「鮑伯」，也是英俚語「先令」的意思。

P. 117　　這時，克瑞奇太太站起身來，她刻意做了打扮，儘管身上的長禮服都改過兩次了，禮服鑲著漂亮的緞帶，那種緞帶很便宜，只要六便士就可以打扮得漂漂亮亮了。她正在鋪桌巾，二女兒貝琳達在一旁幫忙，她也是穿著緞帶鑲邊的衣服。這時候，大兒子彼得拿著叉子插進馬鈴薯的鍋子裡，身上那件大襯衫的衣領頂到了嘴巴（這本來是鮑伯的衣服，為了慶祝今天聖誕節，特地讓給兒子兼繼承人）。他看自己穿得這麼時髦，很是得意，想去時髦人物常去的公園炫耀他的麻布襯衫。

　　此時，克瑞奇家一男一女的兩個小孩衝了進來，他們大聲嚷嚷，說在麵包店外面聞到燒鵝的香味，他們知道那隻鵝是他們家的。兩個孩子沉醉在鼠尾草和洋蔥的奢侈想像中，繞著桌子手舞足蹈，把哥哥彼得捧上了天（但他沒有因此神氣起來，因為衣領勒得他快喘不過氣來），彼得正在吹爐火，直到鍋裡難熟的馬鈴薯噗噗冒泡，打響鍋蓋，才拿出來去皮。

P. 118　　「你們的寶貝父親怎麼啦？還有你們的弟弟小提姆呢？還有瑪莎，去年的聖誕節也只是晚了半個小時。」克瑞奇太太說道。

　　「媽，我回來啦！」一個女孩叫著走進門。

　　「媽媽，瑪莎回來了！」兩個小孩叫嚷著：「呀呼！瑪莎，有一隻這麼大的鵝喔！」

　　「怎麼啦，親愛的，怎麼這麼晚！」克瑞奇太太說著，一邊親吻她了十幾次，慇勤地幫她拿下圍巾和帽子。

　　「媽，昨天晚上我們有好多事要做，今天早上又要做打掃。」女孩回答。

　　「你人回來了就好。親愛的，到爐火前坐下吧，暖暖身體，上帝保佑你！」克瑞奇太太說。

　　「別坐，別坐！爸爸回來了，快躲起來，瑪莎，快躲起來！」兩個小孩大喊，在屋裡四處亂竄。

P.121　　瑪莎趕緊躲起來，爸爸和小鮑伯隨後進門，爸爸圍著流蘇不算在內就超過三呎長的毛織圍巾，垂在前面。為了過節，他一身破舊的衣服已經縫補好刷過，小提姆就坐在他的肩上。可憐的小提姆，他拄著一根小柺杖，雙腿靠鐵架支撐著！

　　「咦，我們的瑪莎呢？」鮑伯四處張望問道。

　　「不回來了。」克瑞奇太太說。

他剛剛才給小提姆當馬騎，
扛著小提姆從教堂一路跑回家。

　　鮑伯說：「不回來了？聖誕節也不回家？」興高采烈的他突然消沉下來。他剛剛才給小提姆當馬騎，扛著小提姆從教堂一路跑回家。

　　就算是開玩笑，瑪莎也不忍心看到他失望的樣子，便提早從壁櫥門後走出來，跑到他的懷裡。兩個小孩則簇擁著小提姆，把他帶到洗衣房，要讓他聽聽布丁在銅鍋裡歌唱的聲音。

　　「小提姆乖不乖呀？」克瑞奇太太問道。她已經取笑過鮑伯，那麼容易就中計。而鮑伯也已經心滿意足地抱過女兒了。

P. 123　　「很乖，難得的乖。不過不知怎麼的，他自己一個人坐著，想了好多，什麼奇怪的事都想。在回家的路上，他對我說，在教堂裡的時候，希望大家都有看到他，因為他跛腳，大家在聖誕節這天看到他，可能會很高興地聯想到是誰讓跛腳的乞丐能走路、讓瞎眼的人看得到東西。」鮑伯說道。

　　鮑伯顫抖著聲音跟大家說這件事情，當他說到小提姆長得愈來愈壯時，聲音顫抖得更厲害了。

　　這時傳來小提姆拄著枴杖靈活走在地板上的聲響，鮑伯正要接著說時，小提姆已經走進來了，由兄姊護送著坐到爐火前的凳子上。這時候，鮑伯捲起袖口（可憐的傢伙，好像在擔心袖口會變得更破舊似的），動手調製混合的熱飲。他把琴酒和檸檬汁倒進一個壺裡，一遍遍攪拌後，再放到爐子上慢慢煮沸。大兒子彼得和那兩個到處亂跑的孩子去拿烤鵝肉，不久就興高采烈地回來了。

接下來一陣嘈雜忙亂的景象，可能會讓你誤以為鵝是最稀罕的飛禽，是長了羽毛的奇蹟，把黑天鵝都比下去了。對這戶人家來說，這的確如此。克瑞奇太太把肉汁加熱煮滾（肉汁已經事先在小長柄鍋裡煮好），大兒子彼得用驚人的力氣把馬鈴薯搗爛，貝琳達小姐在蘋果醬裡加糖，瑪莎把熱盤子擦乾淨；鮑伯把小提姆抱到餐桌旁的小角落，在他旁邊坐下；兩個孩子幫大家把椅子擺好，當然也不會忘記自己的，然後爬上自己的椅子坐好，把湯匙塞進嘴裡，唯恐自己分到鵝肉時會大叫出來。

P. 124 終於，菜都上桌了，禱告詞也唸過了，緊接著大家屏息等待。克瑞奇太太不慌不忙地看著切肉刀，準備插進燒鵝的胸膛。當她一刀戳入，大家期盼已久的內餡湧出來，圍著餐桌響起低聲的歡呼聲，小提姆也受到兩個孩子的影響，用刀柄敲擊桌面，虛弱地喊著：「好耶！」

P. 125　　　真是沒見過這樣的鵝，鮑伯說他不相信鵝可以燒烤得如此美味，肥嫩又鮮美、大隻又便宜，大家同聲稱讚。對這家人來說，燒鵝加上蘋果醬和馬鈴薯泥，夠這一家子人吃了。的確，就像克瑞奇太太看到盤子裡剩下的一小塊骨頭，她開心地說，他們終於有這麼一天，沒有把菜都吃光！大家都已經吃得很飽了，尤其是年幼的那幾個孩子，吃到眉毛上都沾了鼠尾草和洋蔥！這時，貝琳達小姐為大家換上乾淨的盤子，克瑞奇太太獨自離開飯廳，去把布丁從鍋裡拿出來，端進飯廳。她太緊張了，不想讓別人看到布丁完成的樣子。

　　要是布丁沒有蒸熟怎麼辦？要是倒出來的時候破掉了怎麼辦？要是在他們剛才大啖鵝肉的時候，有人翻過後院的牆偷走了布丁，怎麼辦？想到這裡，兩個年幼的孩子臉色都發青了！把各種嚇人的事都想遍了。

　　哎呀！好多蒸氣啊！布丁從銅鍋裡取出來，有洗衣服的味道[5]！那是蒸布的味道，那味道就像餐館和糕餅店比鄰而立，然後隔壁又開了家洗衣店！那是布丁的味道！不一會兒後，克瑞奇太太端著布丁走了進來了（她臉色通紅，得意的笑著）。布丁像一顆斑駁的大砲彈，

5　煮布丁的銅鍋，平時是洗衣服用的。

克瑞奇太太把布丁從鍋裡拿出來，端進飯廳。

飽滿紮實，澆淋了八分之一品脫的白蘭地酒，點上火燃燒著，上面還插著冬青樹枝作裝飾。

P.127　　哇，好棒的布丁啊！鮑伯‧克瑞奇鎮定地說，他覺得這是他們結婚以來做得最成功的布丁。克瑞奇太太說，心上一塊石頭落地了，現在她可以大方承認，她其實是抓不準麵粉的用量的。每個人都對布丁發表了感想，但就是沒有人說（或是覺得），對一個大家庭來說，這布丁是小了一點。要是有人說這種話，就是胡說八道，就算只是稍微暗示一下，都是很難為情的。

　　終於，晚餐結束了。收拾桌布，清理壁爐的爐床，生起爐火。大家嚐了壺裡的熱調酒，覺得無懈可擊。桌上放著蘋果和柳橙，還有滿滿一鏟子的栗子在爐火上烤著。接著，克瑞奇一家人圍著壁爐坐下，鮑伯‧克瑞奇說大家圍成了一個圈，其實是指半個圈。他的手肘邊放著一個平時擺設用的玻璃杯、兩個平底無腳杯，和一個沒有把手的蛋奶凍玻璃杯。

P.129　　這些杯子盛上壺裡倒出來的熱飲，彷彿是用金杯來倒似的。鮑伯眉開眼笑地倒出熱飲，爐火上的栗子發出劈啪的爆裂聲。接著，他舉起酒杯敬酒說：

　　「我親愛的家人，祝大家聖誕節快樂。願上帝保佑我們！」

克瑞奇一家人圍著壁爐坐下

一家人跟著把這句話重複了一遍。

「願上帝保佑我們每一個人！」小提姆最後一個說。

小提姆坐在父親身邊的小凳子上，鮑伯握著他瘦弱的小手，他很疼愛這個小孩，希望把他留在身邊，害怕他會被帶走。

「幽靈，告訴我，小提姆會不會活下來。」史古基問，他以前沒有這樣關心過人。

「我看到冷清的壁爐邊有張椅子沒人坐，還有一根枴杖被保存得好好的，沒有主人。如果這個畫面日後沒有變化，這孩子就是死了。」幽靈回答。

「不，不。哦，不要，好心的幽靈！說他會逃過一劫吧。」史古基說。

P. 131　「如果這個影像日後沒有變化，我們幽靈就不會在這裡再看到他。不過那又怎樣？如果他會死，最好還是死吧，順便好減少過剩的人口。」幽靈答道。

史古基聽見幽靈引用自己說過的話，不禁垂下頭，充滿懊悔與悲傷。

「人啊，如果不是鐵石心腸，就不要說那種惡毒的話，除非你真的知道什麼是人口過剩、哪裡有過剩的人口。你能夠決定誰該活、誰該死嗎？或許在上帝的眼

「願上帝保佑我們每一個人！」

裡，你比千百萬個窮人家的小孩更不值得、更不配活下
去。哦，天啊！你聽聽樹葉上昆蟲說的話，居然說泥土
裡飢餓的兄弟太多了！」

在幽靈的譴責下，史古基低下頭，眼睛看著地
上，顫抖著。不過這時候聽到有人叫自己的名字，他又
很快站直身子。

「史古基先生！我要給史古基先生敬酒，多虧有

他，才有這頓大餐！」鮑伯說。

「多虧有他，才有這頓大餐！真希望他人就在這裡，我要『好好給他一頓招待』，希望他會胃口大開。」克瑞奇太太大聲說道，臉都漲紅了。

P.133　「親愛的，孩子們都在呢！今天是聖誕節呀。」鮑伯說。

「就是在聖誕節這天，我們才會給史古基先生這樣一個可惡、吝嗇、冷酷、無情的人舉杯敬酒。鮑伯，你知道他的為人，沒有人比你更清楚了！可憐的人啊。」她說。

「親愛的，今天是聖誕節。」鮑伯溫和地回答。

「看在你和聖誕節的份上，但不是看在他的份上，我要舉杯敬他身體健康，」瑞奇太太說：「祝他長命百歲！聖誕節快樂，新年快樂！毫無疑問，他一定會幸福快樂。」

孩子們也跟著舉杯敬酒，今天至此，這是他們第一件不熱衷的事情。小提姆最後一個舉杯，冷冷淡淡的。對這家人來說，史古基是凶神惡煞，光是提到他的名字，就會籠罩一層陰影下來，整整五分鐘都不會消散。

等陰影過去之後，因為擺脫了「凶惡史古基」的話題，大家加倍快活了起來。鮑伯·克瑞奇跟大家

「史古基先生！我要給史古基先生敬酒，
　有他，才有這頓大餐！」鮑伯說。

說，他已經幫大兒子彼得相中了一個工作，事情要是能成，週薪足足有五先令六便士。聽到彼得要工作了，兩個小傢伙呵呵大笑。埋頭在襯衫領子的彼得，若有所思地看著爐火，好像在盤算拿到那筆令人眼花撩亂的錢之後，應該要做什麼樣的投資才好。

P. 134　　在女帽店當小學徒的瑪莎，跟大家說自己平時要幹哪些活，一口氣要工作多少個小時，她多麼期盼明天早上可以在床上多睡一會兒。明天放假，她會待在家裡過節。她還說，她前幾天遇到一位伯爵和伯爵夫人，伯爵的個子和彼得差不多高。彼得一聽到這裡，就把衣領拉得老高，你要是在場的話，一定看不到他的頭。他們一邊聊天，栗子和酒壺在大伙間一圈又一圈地傳來遞去。不久，他們聽小提姆唱了首歌，內容是講一個孩子在雪地裡迷了路，歌聲透著哀傷，極為動聽。

　　這裡沒有什麼耀眼的東西，這是個寒酸的家庭，他們沒有好衣服穿，鞋子不防水，衣服單薄，而且彼得很可能去當舖去得很熟了。不過，他們快樂、感恩、相親相愛，很享受共度的時光。幽靈要離開時，從火把灑下明晃晃的星火賜福，讓他們更開心了，然後影像慢慢消逝。史古基看著他們，尤其是盯著小提姆看，直到最後一眼。

　　這時，天色漸暗，雪下得很大，史古基和幽靈沿著街道走，看到家家戶戶的廚房、客廳、各個房間裡燈火通明，很壯觀。這邊，火光閃耀中，看到溫馨的晚餐正張羅著，熱盤子在爐火前烘烤得滾燙，深紅色的窗簾也準備拉上，把寒冷和黑夜隔絕在外。

　　那邊，這家的孩子們衝進大雪中，迎接成家的兄姊、堂表兄姊、叔伯舅舅、姑姑阿姨，爭相要做第一個歡迎他們的人。回到這邊，窗簾上映著賓客歡聚一堂的身影。那邊，一群漂亮的女孩，頭上罩著兜帽、腳下穿著毛皮靴子，一路嘰嘰喳喳地說著話，輕快地跑到附近鄰居的家裡。屋子裡的單身漢看到她們容光煥發地走進來，心裡真是難受啊（這群頑皮的小女巫，她們明白單身漢的心裡是什麼滋味）！

　　若是你看到如此多人出門訪客，你還以為等他們到時，看不到家家戶戶高升爐火，屋子會空蕩蕩的，無人出門迎客。天吶，幽靈樂開懷了！它露出寬闊胸膛，張開巨大手掌，慷慨地向飛過的每片土地，灑下光明和無害的歡笑！

　　那個點燈人沿路將昏暗街道點亮一盞盞燈火，他穿著整整齊齊，打算去哪裡過節了。與幽靈擦身而過時點燈人放聲大笑，只不過他可不知道自己還有聖誕幽靈來作伴呢！

P. 136　此刻，幽靈不說一語兩人便來到一片荒野，四處可見粗獷巨石林立，宛如巨人的墳場。沼地水流處處，要不是被冰雪凍住了，水就會四方竄流。地上只長得出青苔、荊豆和茂盛的粗草。夕陽西沉，一抹火紅的餘暉，像個乖戾的眼睛，瞪視著荒野，眉頭愈皺愈低、愈皺愈低，最後消失在暮色濃重的黑夜裡。

P. 137　「這是什麼地方？」史古基問。

「礦工住的地方。他們在地底下工作，但是他們認識我。你看！」幽靈答道。

一間簡陋小屋的窗子透出光線，他們迅速朝光源走去。穿過泥石砌成的牆後，看到一群人歡聚圍繞在灼灼燃燒的火堆旁。只見一對老邁夫妻和兒孫四代同聚，大家全喜氣洋洋穿著過節的衣裳。老人為眾人唱起了聖誕歌曲，荒野上呼嘯的狂風不時掩蓋過歌聲，那是首古老的歌，從老人兒時便已開始傳唱。大家不時加入一起唱和，大伙一高聲唱和，老人便隨之快活高唱；大家一停，老人的歌聲又再度變小。

幽靈沒有多作停留，它要史古基抓緊它的長袍，接著加速飛越荒野，要飛到哪裡去呢？不會是出海吧？真的出海了。史古基回頭看，不禁一陣驚恐，陸地盡頭那片駭人的岩石被拋在身後。波濤洶湧的浪濤聲讓史古基震耳欲聾，海水不斷翻騰、咆哮著，在海水沖刷而成的可怕岩洞中肆虐，凶猛地侵蝕著陸地。

P. 138　　一座孤寂燈塔矗立在離海岸三、四英里處的荒涼暗礁之上，海浪經年日夜沖刷侵蝕礁石。成堆的海草纏繞在燈塔底座，海燕在四周上下盤旋飛翔（人們可能不禁會以為海燕生於風，就如海草生於海中），而鳥兒飛掠而過的海浪也忽上忽下地翻騰著。

　　即便是在這裡，兩個看守燈塔的人也生起了火，火光從粗厚石牆的縫隙流瀉而出，照射在恐怖的海面上。他們坐在粗陋的桌子旁，握住對方長繭的手，舉酒互相祝聖誕快樂。其中年長的那位，臉上在嚴酷天候的摧殘下瘢痕累累、風霜滿面，就像老舊船頭上裝飾的人像。他唱起雄壯的曲子，悍如外頭呼嘯的狂風。

　　幽靈再次快速前進，在漆黑洶湧的海上飛行，飛啊飛，一直到幽靈跟史古基說，四周離海岸已經很遙遠了，才落在一艘船上。他們站在舵手旁邊，一旁還有船尾的瞭望人、幾位負責值班的船員，鬼魅般的黑暗身影堅守在各自的崗位上，每個人哼著聖誕歌曲，想著聖誕節的種種，也有人跟同伴輕聲聊起往年的聖誕節，心念著回鄉過節。這一天，船上的人人，不管醒著、睡著，脾氣是好、是壞，都會比平日多說些好話，分享一下過節的氣氛，思念起遠方所掛念的人，也知道對方會開心地想起自己。

P. 139　　聽著海風怒號，史古基吃驚地想著，在這孤寂的黑暗中航行前進，橫渡如死亡般深不可測的未知深淵，是一件多麼嚴肅的事啊！這時，一個歡笑聲嚇到了思緒中的史古基，史古基認出來那是外甥的笑聲之後更是吃驚，他發現自己置身一間明亮、乾爽、燈火通明的房間裡。幽靈微笑地站在一旁，用和藹可親的讚許神情，看著他的外甥！

　　「哈，哈！哈，哈，哈！」史古基的外甥大笑著。

　　儘管不太可能，不過要是你不巧認識了有誰比史古基的外甥更會笑的人，我真想說我也想認識他，把他介紹給我吧，我要交他這個朋友。

P. 140　　世事的安排，公道又高明。雖然疾病和悲傷會傳染，但這世界上最具感染力、令人難以抗拒的，是笑聲和愉快的心情。史古基的外甥抱著腰、搖著頭大笑，一張臉扭曲到最誇張的程度，外甥媳也一樣笑翻了，一群朋友也不甘示弱地縱聲狂笑。

　　「哈，哈！哈，哈，哈！」

　　「千真萬確！他說聖誕節是鬼扯淡，他真的這麼認為！」外甥大聲說道。

　　「那真是太難為情了，弗瑞德！」外甥媳憤慨地說道。上帝保佑這些女人吧，她們做事情從不會打馬虎眼，什麼事都很當真。

　　她人很美，美極了。美麗的臉龐帶著酒窩，神情生動，一張嫣紅的小嘴，好像生來就是要讓人一親芳澤的，毫無疑問。下巴迷人的小雀斑，在她笑起時融合為一。還有那雙你在別人身上見不到的閃耀眸子。總之，她是那種令人怦然心動、滿意不已的女子。哦，滿意的不得了！

P. 141　　「他真是個好笑的老傢伙，我是說真的，只不過他可以更討人喜歡的。他自作自受，沒有什麼好去說他的。」外甥說道。

　　「弗瑞德，他一定很有錢，至少你都是這麼對我說的。」外甥媳暗示道。

　　「親愛的，那又怎麼樣呢？財富對他來說是沒有用處的，他的錢不會拿來行善，也不會拿來讓自己過得舒服一點。他只要一想到，哈，哈，哈！他的錢以後會庇蔭我們，就一點也不快樂了。」外甥說道。

　　「我實在受不了他。」外甥媳說。她的姊妹們和現場的女士們也都同聲附和道。

「哦，我可以！我為他感到難過，就算我要生他的氣，也氣不起來。誰會因為他的壞脾氣而難受？只有他自己。他打定主意不喜歡我們，不願來我們這裡一起圍爐。結果怎麼樣呢？他並不差這一頓飯。」外甥說。

「我倒覺得他錯過了一頓很豐盛的晚餐。」外甥媳插嘴說道，大夥也應聲附和。大家說的是公道話，因為他們才剛享用過晚餐，桌上現在還擺著甜點，大家在燈火下圍爐而坐。

P. 142　「喔！很高興聽到這句話，因為我對這些年輕的家庭主婦不太有信心。托普，你覺得呢？」外甥說。

很顯然，托普看上了外甥媳的一個妹妹，因為他回答說，單身漢就像可憐的流浪漢，沒有資格發表意見。這位妹妹一聽，臉就紅了。是那一位身材豐腴、穿著蕾絲領紗的妹妹，而不是戴玫瑰花的那一位。

「繼續說呀，弗瑞德。」外甥媳鼓掌說道：「這奇怪的傢伙都不把話講完！」

外甥又開心地大笑起來，笑聲的感染力似乎無人能擋。那位豐腴妹妹聞著芳香醋[6]，想忍住不笑出來，結果還是跟著大家笑出來了。

6　芳香療法，用來預防頭痛。

外甥說：「我只想說，他不喜歡我們、不和我們一起同樂，損失的是快樂的時光，而快樂是不會害到他的。我敢說，不管是在他發霉的舊辦公室裡，或是在他布滿灰塵的房間裡，他都想不出可以去哪裡找這麼好作伴的人了。我很同情他，所以不管他喜不喜歡，我每年都會去邀請他。也許他到死都會埋怨聖誕節，但是我敢說，如果他發現我年復一年都去找他，好聲好氣地對他說：『史古基舅舅，你好嗎？』我想他也會忍不住往好的一面想。只要能讓他想到，將來可以留個五十鎊給他那個可憐的文書員，那就很了不起了。我覺得我昨天有打動到他了。」

P. 143　　現在輪到他們大笑起來了，竟然會有打動史古基的妄想。不過他脾氣可好了，隨便大家笑什麼都行，任大夥去笑。他要大家盡情歡樂，開心地把酒瓶傳下去。

喝完茶以後，他們來了點音樂。這家人喜愛音樂，不論是合唱還是輪唱，我保證他們都知道自己在唱什麼。特別是托普，他的男低音可不是蓋的，大聲地嗚嗚唱去，額頭上既不會冒青筋，也不會憋紅一張臉。

外甥媳的豎琴彈得很好，她彈了幾首曲子，有一首是簡單的小調（很簡單的調子，學個兩分鐘就能用口哨吹出來）。先前，「往日聖誕幽靈」帶史古基回到過去的時候，到史古基的寄宿學校接他回家的小女孩，也很熟悉這個調子。

P. 144　當小調的樂音一響起，幽靈之前帶領史古基看過的昔日畫面，一一浮現腦海。他的心逐漸軟化下來，他心想，要是幾年前能多聽這首曲子，他可能會活得比較仁慈，能夠親手創造自己的幸福，而非親手拿著教堂執事的鐵鍬來埋葬雅各‧馬里。

他們並沒有整晚都在唱歌。不久大夥玩起了罰物遊戲，有時回頭當當小孩也不錯，而聖誕節就是最佳時機了，因為在這天，偉大的創造者自己也是個小孩。

慢著！他們先玩起蒙眼捉迷藏遊戲，當然要玩這個了。就像我不相信托普的靴子長了眼睛，我壓根才不相信他真的看不見。我認為他和史古基的外甥早就串通好了，而幽靈也知道這麼回事。看他追逐那個蕾絲領紗豐腴妹妹的模樣，簡直就冒犯了對人性的信任。他撞倒了撥火鉗、被椅子絆倒、撞上鋼琴，鑽到窗簾後面，還差點把自己悶死，不過不管她躲到哪裡，他都如影隨形，不管怎樣就會知道她躲在哪裡。他不會抓別人，要是你故意擋住他（他們幾個人確實也這樣做了），他會假裝要抓你，但是那對於你的智慧是一種侮辱，因為他會馬上側身朝豐腴妹妹追去。

P. 146 　　她不停地叫這不公平。這確實不公平，不過最後他還是抓到她了，儘管她飛快地閃躲，絲綢衣服窸窣作聲，卻還被他逼到角落，無處可逃。此刻他的舉動才是極盡惡劣，因為他裝作不知道抓到誰，還得摸摸她的頭飾，摸摸她手指上的戒指、頸上的項鍊，才認得出她是誰。這簡直卑鄙無恥！等換別人當鬼時，她肯定跟他說了自己的想法，兩個人就親密地躲在窗簾後說起了悄悄話。

　　史古基的外甥媳沒有玩捉迷藏遊戲，而是找了個舒適的角落，愜意地坐在大椅子上，雙腿擱在腳凳上，而幽靈和史古基就緊跟在她身後。不過她玩了罰物遊戲，還有用所有字母開頭造句道出對心上人的讚美。在玩「猜字遊戲」的時候，她一樣表現出色。外甥暗自得意，因為她把姊妹們打得落花流水。不過，她的姐妹們可也是個個無比聰明的，這一點，托普可以告訴你。

P. 147 　　那裡約莫有二十個人，老老少少，眾人都下場玩遊戲，就連史古基也玩了起來。他玩得太入迷，忘了他們聽不見他的聲音，有好幾次大聲說出自己猜出的答案，而且往往還猜中。因為就算是保證不會從針眼處斷掉、最尖銳的「白教堂」牌縫衣針，也比不上史古基心思銳利，雖然他常自認為自己很遲鈍。

他追逐穿著蕾絲領紗的豐腴妹妹

他還是把她逼到屋角，無處可逃。

看到史古基心情這麼好，幽靈很欣慰。他像小男孩那樣央求留到散會，幽靈很歡心地看著他。只不過，幽靈說它愛莫能助。

「又有新遊戲了，再待半個小時，幽靈，一個遊戲就好！」史古基說。

這個遊戲叫做「對與錯」，外甥的心裡要想著一樣東西，然後讓其他人去猜。其他人會發問，外甥只能按照事實去回答「對」或「錯」。大家連珠砲地發問，問出來他心裡想的是一種動物，活的，令人退避三舍，很野蠻，有時會咆哮喔喔叫，有時會講話，住在倫敦，在大街小巷走動，不會被送去展覽拍賣，不必人牽，不住在動物園，不會被送去市場宰殺掉，不是馬，不是驢子，不是母牛，不是公牛，不是老虎，不是狗，不是豬，不是貓，不是熊。

P. 148　大家每問他一次，外甥就會哈哈大笑，笑到受不了了，就從沙發上站起來跺腳。最後，豐腴的妹妹也著笑個不停，大聲說道：

「我知道答案了！弗瑞德，我知道答案是什麼了！我知道答案是什麼了！」

「是什麼？」弗瑞德問。

「是你舅舅，史──古──基！」

答案完全正確。大家都稱讚她，雖然有人抗議說，剛剛問是不是熊[7]的時候，就應該要回答「對」，不然會誤導大家，因為有人可能已經快要聯想到史古基了。

P. 150 「看來他已經帶給我們很多歡樂了，好歹敬他的健康一杯吧。現在我們就用手邊的香料熱紅酒，來吧，敬史古基舅舅！」弗瑞德說道。

「敬史古基舅舅！」他們喊道。

「不管他是什麼樣的人，祝老人家聖誕快樂、新年快樂！」外甥說：「雖然他不接受我的祝福，但我還是希望他能得到我的祝福。敬史古基舅舅！」

史古基舅舅不知不覺已經變得心情輕鬆快活，如果幽靈能給他時間，他一定會回敬這些不知道他在場、也聽不到他說話的人，並且跟他們道謝。但是，等外甥說完最後一個字，眼前情景就消失了，他和幽靈再度繼續前進。

他們看了很多東西，去了很遠的地方，到了很多人家的家裡，處處都是圓滿收場。幽靈站在病床旁，病人的精神就好起來；到了異鄉，遊子們便感覺離家很近；奮鬥掙扎的人，變得有耐心與希望；窮苦人家也覺

7　熊（bear）也可指粗魯、不禮貌的人。

大家每問他一次，外甥就會哈哈大笑，
笑到受不了了，就從沙發上站起來跺腳。

得變富有了。他們去了救濟院、醫院、監獄、苦命人的庇護所，只要那個有些小權勢、自命不凡的掌權人沒有把大門深鎖，將幽靈擋在門外，幽靈都會留下祝福，順便跟史古基說些道理。

P. 151 雖然那只是一晚，這晚卻感覺長夜漫漫。但史古基心生懷疑，因為好像整個聖誕假期都濃縮他和幽靈一起度過的這段時光裡了。還有一件事也很奇怪，史古基外貌並沒有改變，但幽靈卻明顯變老了。史古基只是看在眼裡，沒有說出口，直到他們離開一個為孩子們舉辦的主顯節晚會，一起站在外面，史古基看著幽靈才發現它的頭髮已經花白了。

「幽靈的壽命很短嗎？」史古基問。

「我在這個世上的生命很短，今晚就會結束了。」幽靈回答。

「今晚！」史古基嘆道。

「今晚十二點。你聽！時間快到了。」

這時響起了十一點四十五分的鐘聲。

「恕我冒昧，或許我不該問，」史古基盯著著幽靈的長袍說。「不過我看到不該是你身上的怪東西從長袍下伸出來，那是腳還是爪子？」

P. 152 「從上面的肉來看，可能是爪子。」幽靈哀傷地

答道：「你看這裡。」

長袍的皺褶裡，出來了兩個小孩，一副可憐、悲慘、恐懼、醜陋、痛苦的樣子。他們跪在幽靈的腳邊，緊抓著長袍的外邊。

「噢，天啊！你看這裡。你看，看下面這裡！」幽靈大叫著。

那是一個小男孩和一個小女孩，他們面黃肌瘦、衣衫襤褸、板著一張臉、惡狠狠的，卻又卑躬屈膝地趴伏在地上。原本應該是青春洋溢的模樣，卻像是剛被一隻骯髒、皺巴巴的大人的手給染指了，他們的面貌被擠壓、扭絞，被摧殘得不成人形。他們本該被天使捧坐在寶座上，卻被惡魔纏身，睜大恫嚇的雙眼。一切奧妙的生靈中，人再怎麼改變、墮落、扭曲，駭人的程度都不及這怪物的一半。

史古基嚇得往後退，一陣毛骨悚然。見到他們這副模樣，原本想說他們是漂亮的孩子，話卻卡在喉嚨，撒不了這種漫天大謊。

P. 153

「幽靈！他們是你的小孩嗎？」史古基實在說不出別的話來。

「他們是人類的小孩。」幽靈低頭看著他們，說道：「他們緊跟著我不放，是他們的祖先要他們來求情的。這個男孩叫『無知』，女孩叫『貧乏』。要當心他們兩個，還有他們的同類，尤其要小心男孩，他的額頭上寫著『滅亡』兩個字，字不擦掉的話，就會滅亡。」幽靈伸直手臂，指著倫敦那座城市說：「儘管不以為然吧！儘管毀謗預言這件事的人吧！如果是別有存心才承認這種事，那情況只會變本加厲，等著承擔後果吧！」

「沒有人可以收留或是幫助他們嗎？」史古基說。

「難道沒有監獄嗎？」幽靈說道。它最後一次轉身看著史古基，用史古基曾說過的話回答：「難道沒有勞動濟貧所嗎？」

這時，鐘聲敲響十二下。

史古基環顧四周，尋找著幽靈，可是幽靈已經消失不見。等最後一聲響完，他想起了老雅各‧馬里的預言。他抬起眼，看到一個神容蕭穆的幽靈，披著斗篷、披著斗蓬，像地面上的霧氣般朝他緩緩飄來。

這個男孩叫「無知」，女孩叫「貧乏」。

第四樂章

最後一個幽靈

P. 154 幽靈肅穆無聲地緩緩飄來。當它飄近時，史古基屈膝跪了下來，因為幽靈一飄過，空氣中就瀰漫著陰森詭祕的氣氛。

幽靈身上披著暗黑色的斗篷，把頭、臉和身體都遮住，除了伸出的一隻手，什麼都遮住看不到。要不是有那隻手伸出來，夜裡很難分辨出幽靈的身影，也難以把它和四周黑漆漆的黑夜區隔開來。

幽靈來到史古基的身邊，他覺得幽靈威嚴高大。幽靈詭祕的出現，讓他一陣深沉的恐懼。他毫無頭緒，因為幽靈一語不發，一動也不動。

「在我眼前的是『來日聖誕幽靈』嗎？」史古基問道。

P. 156 幽靈沒有回答，只是用手指向前方。

「你是要給我看那些尚未發生、但即將發生的事，是嗎，幽靈？」史古基又問。

幽靈沒有回答，只是用手指向前方。

斗篷上半部的皺摺縮動了一下，看起來像是幽靈點了點頭。這是他得到的唯一回應。

儘管到現在史古基已經很習慣和幽靈結伴同行，但這沉默鬼影仍讓他驚恐不已，雙腳打顫。他準備跟幽靈走時發現自己站不穩腳。幽靈看到他的樣子就停下來，等他恢復過來。

不料這樣史古基反倒更驚慌了。只覺一股莫名深刻的恐懼，他知道在灰暗的裹屍衣下，有一雙鬼眼正盯著他看。不管他再怎麼用力睜眼，還是只看到一隻鬼手和一團高大的黑影。

「來日幽靈啊！你比我見過的其他幽靈都更令我害怕。不過我知道你是為了我好才來的，而我也想洗心革面，所以我懷著感恩的心，準備跟你走，可是你怎麼不和我說話呢？」他喊道。

P. 157 幽靈還是沒有回答，只把手直直地指向他們的前方。

「帶路吧！帶路吧！晚上時間過得很快，時間對我來說是很寶貴的，我知道。就帶路吧，幽靈！」史古基說。

幽靈就像剛才朝他飄過來那樣又飄走，史古基跟在斗篷的影子後面，他感覺影子把他托了起來，帶著他一路前行。

　　他們似乎不像是進了城，反倒像是城市倏然湧現眼前將他們包圍住。他們已來到市中心，身處證券交易所裡的忙進忙出的商人群中，商人口袋裡的錢幣叮噹作響，三三兩兩地交頭接耳。他們看看手錶，一面把玩著的大金印，心頭一面盤算著。這等事都是史古基再熟悉不過的場景了。

　　幽靈停在幾個商人的旁邊，史古基看到幽靈的手指著他們，便走上前聽他們談話。

　　「這件事我也不清楚，我只知道他死了。」一個

下巴寬大的大胖子說道。

P. 159　「他是什麼時候死的？」另一個人問。

　　「我想，應該是昨天晚上吧。」

　　「為什麼？他是出了什麼事啊？」另一個問，他從大鼻菸盒大力吸了一口，「我還以為他永遠死不了！」

　　「天曉得出了什麼事。」第一個人說著打了個呵欠。

　　「那他怎麼處理他的錢？」一個滿面紅光的紳士問道，他的鼻尖垂著一顆肉瘤，像公火雞下顎的垂肉那樣晃來晃去。

　　「沒聽說，可能是留給公司吧，我只知道沒有留給我。」下巴寬大的那個男的說著又打了呵欠。

　　這句話惹得大家哄堂大笑。

　　「葬禮會辦得很便宜吧。我敢說，沒有人會去送殯，我們要不要找些人一起去送他？」那個人又說。

　　「要是有供應午餐，我倒是可以去。」鼻尖垂肉瘤的紳士說：「要有吃的，我才要去。」

　　又是一陣大笑。

　　「這我沒興趣，我不戴喪禮的黑手套，也不吃喪禮的午餐。不過要是有人要去，我就跟著去。想一

340

想，我可能算是他最好的朋友吧，我們每次碰面時，都
會停下來聊幾句。再見了！」第一個說話的人說。

P. 161　　這群敘話的人散開後，又找別人閒聊去了。這些
人史古基都認識，他看著幽靈，想聽幽靈說明是怎麼一
回事。

　　幽靈飄到街上，手指指向兩個不期而遇的人，史
古基又繼續聽他們談什麼，想聽出個所以然。

　　這兩人他也很熟。他們是生意人，有錢有勢。他

一向努力想得到這兩個人的敬重，當然了，是純粹從做生意的立場出發。

「您好。」一個人說。

「您好。」另一個人回答。

「那個老鬼總算走了吧？」第一個說。

「聽說了。」第二個人回：「好冷啊！是吧？」

「聖誕節就是這樣！我想你不會要去溜冰吧？」

「不，不。我還有事，我先走了！」

再沒別的話了，他們碰面就這聊了幾句話，就分開了。

P. 162　　一開始史古基覺得奇怪，幽靈怎麼會覺得這等瑣碎談話很重要，但他又覺得一定另有深意，便琢磨著幽靈的用意。他們說的應該和舊合夥人雅各的死無關，因為那是「過去」的事，而這幽靈是管「未來」之事。他想不透任何與自己有關的人會和他們的談話內容沾上邊。但無疑地，不管話中牽扯到誰，都是要來助他改頭換面的。他決意要牢記所聽所見到的一切，尤其是當未來自己的身影現身時更要多加留意。因為他期待看到未來自己的言行之後，就能發現他之前遺漏的線索，輕易解開這些謎團。

史古基四處尋看未來的自己，卻只見自己習慣站

著的那角落站著另一個人。時鐘顯示的時間是他平常
會出現的時刻，可是湧進交易所門廊的那一大批人潮
中，他看不見相似自己的身影。不過，他對此也不是太
驚訝，因為他已經決心要重新做人，希望看到的是煥然
一新的自己。

P. 163　　四周沉靜暗黑，幽靈站在他身邊，伸出一隻手。
當他從沉思中回神過來時，從幽靈那隻手轉動的方
向，還有幽靈和他的相對位置來看，史古基猜想那雙看
不見的眼睛正銳利地盯著他看，他不禁不寒而慄，渾身
發寒。

　　他們離開繁忙的街角，來到城裡一個偏僻晦暗地
區。史古基沒有來過這裡，不過倒知道這地方臭名昭
彰。街道髒亂狹窄，店舖住家破舊，人們衣衫不整，喝
得醉茫茫的，懶懶散散，醜態畢露。巷弄四處可見穢
物，把臭味、垃圾、惡氣都吐到髒亂不堪的街道上，整
個地區充斥著犯罪、污穢和窮困。

　　他們深入這塊惡名昭彰的地區，來到一間閣樓屋
簷下的店，店門面低矮突出到街上。這家店專收鐵製
品、舊衣服、瓶瓶罐罐、動物骨頭和油膩膩的內臟。店
裡地板上堆滿了生鏽的鑰匙、鐵釘、鏈子、鉸鏈、銼
刀、磅秤、秤砣，什麼破銅爛鐵都有。沒有人想去挖掘

的祕密，就藏在堆積如山的破布、大量腐敗的油脂和屍骨中。

P. 164
一個頭髮灰白、年近七十的無賴漢，就坐在這堆待售的物品中，身旁還有個舊磚砌煤爐。他把各種臭破布掛在一根繩子上當成簾子，用來阻隔外面的寒風，在裡面悠哉地抽著菸斗。

史古基和幽靈走到老頭面前，剛好有個婦人拿著沉重的包袱偷偷摸摸地溜進店裡，她才一踏進門，另個女人也拿著包袱進門，後頭緊跟著一個身穿褪色黑衣的男人，見著那兩個女人大吃一驚，就像兩個女人認出對方一樣嚇得目瞪口呆。三個人都呆住了，抽菸斗的老人見狀也是一陣吃驚，三人不禁大笑了起來。

第一個進來的女人說：「讓我這個幫傭的先來吧！洗衣婦排第二，葬儀社的人排第三。你看看，老喬，就這麼巧！我們三個人可沒有約好在這裡碰面！」

P. 165
「你們算是來對地方了，到客廳吧！」老喬把菸斗從嘴上拿下說：「我說啊，你早就對這兒熟門熟路了，另外兩位也不算陌生。等我先把店門關起來再說。噢！這門的聲音可真刺耳！我敢說店裡生鏽得最厲害的鐵器就是這門鉸鏈了。店裡最老的骨頭也就我這把老骨頭了吧！哈，哈！我們可幹對這一行了，真是絕配了。到客廳吧，到客廳來。」

　　說是客廳就在那破布廉後面。老喬拿起一根舊樓梯毯壓條耙了耙爐火，又用菸斗柄調整了一下冒黑煙的燈蕊（當時是晚上），再放回嘴裡。

　　老喬一邊忙著，方才開口的婦人把包袱扔地上，炫耀似地坐在板凳上。兩手交叉擱在膝蓋上，囂張地盯著另外兩個人看。

　　「這有什麼要緊的？狄柏太太，當然了，每個人都有權為自己打算，『他』以前就是這樣啊！」那女人說。

P. 166　　「是啊，沒錯！沒人比他更在行了。」洗衣婦說道。

　　「那你這女人就不要站在那裡瞪著眼，好像在怕什麼似的。誰會曉得啊？我們不會互相揭穿吧？」

　　「不會，當然不會！我們都不希望這樣。」狄柏太太和男人同聲說道。

　　「那很好！這就夠了，誰會在乎沒了這幾樣東西呢？尤其死人更不會吧。」那女人說。

　　「那還用說！」狄柏太太笑著說。

　　「那個缺德的守財奴要是想死後保有這些東西，

怎麼生前不對人好一點？」女人接著說：「那他斷氣時身邊至少會有人照顧他，不會一個人孤伶伶地躺在那裡，嚥下最後一口氣。」

「你話倒說得很實在，這是他的報應。」狄柏太太說。

「我倒希望他再多一點報應，要是能多拿點東西，我鐵定不客氣。老喬，打開那包東西吧，看看值多少錢，爽快開個價吧！我不怕當第一個，也不怕讓他們看見。相信來這裡前，我們心裡都有數這些都是不告而取的。這可不是什麼罪。老喬，打開包袱吧。」女人說。

P. 167 另外兩人也不讓她專美於前。身穿舊黑衣的男人率先亮出他摸來的東西，沒幾樣，只有一兩個印章、一個鉛筆盒、一對袖扣、一個沒什麼價值的胸針，就這些。老喬一樣樣仔細查看估價，用粉筆把每樣東西的收購價錢一一寫在牆上，等到都估價完了，再把總數加起來。

「這是這個價，就算把我丟進油鍋，我也不會多給你六便士。下一個換誰？」老喬說。

接下來是狄柏太太。幾條床單和毛巾、幾件衣服、兩支舊式銀茶匙、一把方糖夾子和幾雙靴子。她的報價也一樣用粉筆寫在牆上。

「你說這是什麼？」喬說：「床帳？」

「我老是給女人出價太高，這是我的弱點，會毀了自己。這是你的價，你要我再多加一便士，跟我討價還價，我可要後悔自己太大方，扣妳半克朗了。」老喬說。

P. 168　「喬，現在打開我的包袱吧。」第一個女人說。

喬跪下來好方便打開包袱，好不容易解開了幾個結後，拖出一大捲重重的深色東西。

「你說這是什麼？」喬問他：「是床帳？」

「噢！」婦人雙臂交叉胸前，身體前傾，笑著說，「沒錯，就是床帳！」

「該不會他還躺在那裡時，你就把床帳連掛鉤什麼的都扯了下來吧？」喬說。

「沒錯！不行嗎？」女人答。

「你天生就是要吃這口飯的，不賺不行。」喬說。

「喬，我敢說，對於『他』這種人更不必客氣，既然伸手有東西拿，自然就不必縮手。」那女人冷冷地說：「別把燈油滴到毯子上了。」

「那是他的毯子？」喬問。

「不然還會是誰的？我敢說他現在少了這些毯子也不會著涼的。」女人回。

「他該不會死於什麼傳染病吧？」老喬停下來，抬頭問道。

P. 170　「這你大可放心。」婦人回答說：「我才不喜歡陪他，要是他有傳染病，我才不會為了這些東西守在他身邊。啊！你大可仔細檢查那件襯衫，就算你把眼睛看到酸痛了也找不出破洞或磨損的地方。那是他最好的襯衫，很高檔，要不是我，就會被他們糟蹋掉了。」

「你說糟蹋，是什麼意思？」老喬問道。

「他們要讓他穿著下葬。」女人笑答：「有人傻到要讓他穿上，我趕緊把它脫下來。白棉布襯衫就夠好的了，何必浪費？而且他穿起來很合身，也沒有更醜。」

史古基驚恐地聽著他們談話。在老頭那盞微弱的燈火下，他們圍坐在贓物的四周，史古基看著他們，感到深痛惡絕，好像他們是一群販賣屍首的無恥惡魔。

這時老喬拿出一個裝著錢的法蘭絨袋，把他們該拿的錢數出來放地上。女人笑著說道，「你們看，這就是下場！他生前把身邊的人都嚇跑了；死了倒是便宜了我們！哈，哈，哈！」

P. 171　「幽靈！我懂了，我懂了！」史古基渾身顫抖地說：「我的下場可能就跟這個倒霉鬼一樣，我的人生就是那樣子過的。天啊，這又是什麼？」

　　眼前的景象又變了，他嚇得往後退，差點碰到了一張床。床空空的沒有床帳遮蔽，只有個破舊的床單蓋住什麼東西，儘管無聲無息，卻用一種可怕的言語聲明自己的存在。

　　房間裡很暗，什麼都看不清楚。史古基環顧四周，有股莫明衝動急切地想搞清楚房間是什麼樣子。外頭一道微弱的光線正照射床舖上，床上躺著的遺體被人洗劫一空，沒人看管，沒人哭泣，沒人照料。

　　史古基望了幽靈一眼，幽靈的手沉穩地指著屍體的頭。舊床單只是隨意蓋上去的，史古基只消動一動手指，輕輕一掀，那張臉就會露出來。他想了想，知道這很容易，也渴望動手，但就是沒膽掀開床單，就像他沒有膽子趕走身邊的幽靈。

P. 172　　哦，冷酷、冷酷、嚴峻、可怕的死神啊！竟把祭壇設在了這裡，用這種你能支配的恐怖力量來當裝飾，因為這是你的地盤！而那些受人喜愛、尊敬、景仰的人，你就動不了他一根汗毛，也無法把他變得醜惡。儘管他的手變得沉重，一放手就會掉下去，心臟和脈搏也停止了，但那隻手生前大方、慷慨、忠誠，他的內心勇敢、熱忱溫柔，心跳也如常人脈動。來吧，死

神，來吧！你會看到他的善行從傷口裡湧出，以不朽的
生命將善行散播於世上！

P. 173 　　沒有人在史古基的耳邊說話，但當他望著床上時
卻聽見了聲音。他想，如果這個人現在復活了，第一個
浮現的念頭是什麼？是貪婪？是商場上的爾虞我詐與盤
算？的確，就是這些念頭才會讓他最後落得如此下場！

　　他躺在陰暗的空屋裡，見不到任何男女老幼在旁
說「他生前如何善待我」、「我記得他曾跟我說過什麼

史古基沒有膽子去掀開床單，
就像他沒有膽子趕走身邊的幽靈。

好話，我要好好送他」。有隻貓正抓著門板，爐磚下面傳來老鼠齧咬的聲音，牠們想在這個躺著死人的房間裡找什麼？為什麼這樣躁動不安？史古基不敢想下去。

「幽靈！這地方太可怕了。離開這裡後，我一定不會忘記得到的教訓，相信我，我們走吧！」他說。

幽靈的手仍一動也不動地指著那個頭。

「我知道你的意思，我願意照辦，但是我不敢，幽靈，我不敢。」史古基答道。

P. 174 精靈似乎又在盯著他看。

「假如城裡有誰替這個人的死傷心難過，那就帶我去看看他吧。幽靈，我求你了！」史古基痛苦地說。

幽靈在史古基面前把黑色的長袍一揮，像展翅一樣，長袍放下的片刻，眼前出現了一間明亮的房間，有位母親和孩子們在屋內。

看來她正焦急地等人，在房間來回踱步，一點聲響都會驚嚇到她。她不時望向窗外，看看時鐘，想做點針線活又做不下去，連孩子們的嬉鬧聲也讓她受不了。

終於，傳來了敲門聲，她急忙跑到門口去迎接丈夫。他的臉還很年輕，但顯得飽經憂患。此刻他的臉露出奇特的神情，一種他難以掩藏的喜悅，但又恥於自己流露出愉悅而極力壓抑著。

　　他坐下來吃晚餐，飯菜一直放在爐火旁溫著。沉默半晌之後，妻子小聲問起丈夫有什麼消息，丈夫一臉尷尬，難以啟齒的樣子。

P. 175　　「是好消息，還是壞消息？」妻子幫他起頭開口。

　　「壞消息。」他答道。

　　「我們是不是完蛋了？」

　　「不會的，凱洛琳，還是有希望的。」

　　「他要是能大發慈悲，那就有希望了！」她驚訝地說：「如果天底下有這種奇蹟，那什麼事都有希望了。」

　　「他沒辦法大發慈悲了，」丈夫說：「他死了。」

　　如果她的表情流露出實情，那她倒可算是個溫和又有耐性的人。但聽到這消息她只想謝天謝地，緊握雙手說出了自己內心的感受。但在下一刻她祈求上帝恕罪，並為死亡感到難過，只不過她一開始的反應才是她真正的心聲。

　　「昨晚我去找他，想求他寬限一個星期還錢。當時是那個喝得半醉的女人告訴我的，我還以為那只是個打發我的藉口，誰想到是真的。他那時不只病重，根本就快死了。」

　　「那我們欠的債以後要還給誰？」

「我不知道。不過到那時我們就能備好錢了，就算錢沒有籌好，他的債權繼承人又如他一般冷酷，也就這樣了。凱洛琳，至少我們今晚可以好好睡一覺了！」

P. 176 的確，狀況解除了，心情也輕鬆不少。孩子們安靜地圍著父母聽著這些似懂非懂的事，臉上卻也更活潑開朗了。這人的死竟帶給這一家子歡樂！幽靈讓他看到，眾人對這人的死，居然只有喜悅之情。

「幽靈，讓我看看那些憐憫死者的人吧，不然我們剛剛離開的那個陰暗房間，會在我眼前永遠揮之不去。」史古基說。

幽靈帶著他走過幾條熟悉的街道。沿途史古基一直四處張望尋找著自己的身影，卻無處可尋。他們走進可憐的鮑伯・克瑞奇的家，之前他曾來過這裡，看見母親和孩子們圍爐而坐。

屋內靜悄悄的，鴉雀無聲。兩個愛嬉鬧的小鬼待在角落邊，安靜得像雕像，坐著抬頭望著彼得，他面前擺了一本書。母親和女兒正做著針線活，但她們真的都太安靜了！

「『於是領過一個小孩子來，叫他站在門徒中間。』[1]」

史古基是在哪裡聽過這句話的？他沒在作夢，一定是他和幽靈跨進門時那男孩唸出來的。他怎麼不唸下去了呢？

P. 177 　　母親把針線活放在桌上，用手蒙著臉。

　　「這顏色讓我的眼睛好痛。」她說。

　　顏色？噢，可憐的小提姆！[2]

　　「現在好多了。燭光傷眼，不管了，我可不願你們父親回家看到我的眼睛不好。他差不多要到家了吧。」克瑞奇太太說。

　　「時間早就超過了。媽媽，我覺得最近這幾個晚上他走得比平常慢。」彼得把書闔起來說道。

　　他們又陷入一陣靜默。終於，她開口說話，聲音沉穩有活力，只是中間頓了一下：

　　「我知道他以前——以前會讓小提姆坐在肩膀上，就走得很快。」

　　「我也知道，他常常這樣。」彼得說。

P. 178 　　「我也知道！」又有人喊道，大家也都跟應聲。

　　母親接著說：「不過他背起來很輕，」她又專心做起針線活，「而且爸爸那麼愛他，一點也不嫌麻

1　出自《聖經·馬可福音》第九章第36節。
2　指黑色，因為小提姆過世了，他們在縫製喪服。

煩，一點也不麻煩。你們的爸爸到家門口了！」

她急忙跑出去迎接，小鮑伯脖子上圍著那條長圍巾走進門（他需要這玩意，可憐的傢伙）。他的茶早就泡好放爐上，大家爭相幫他倒茶。接著那兩個小鬼爬到他的膝上，窩在他的懷裡，把小臉蛋貼在他的臉頰上，一邊一個，好像在說：「別難過，爸爸，別傷心了！」

鮑伯和他們在一起很開心，高高興興地跟全家人聊天。他看著桌上的針線活，稱讚太太和女兒很勤快。他說，看樣子不必等星期天就可以做完了。

「星期天！鮑伯，這麼說來你今天去過了？」妻子問。

「是啊，親愛的。」鮑伯回答，「真希望你也去，那地方一片綠意盎然，你一定會很喜歡的。你以後會常去的。我答應過他，每個星期天都會去看他。我的小兒子啊！」鮑伯哭道。

P. 179　鮑伯突然崩潰，再也無法克制自己。如果他能忍住，也許他和兒子就沒那麼親近了。

他離開客廳到樓上房間，房裡光線明亮，四處掛滿聖誕飾品。孩子的身邊擺了一張椅子，看來不久前有人坐過。可憐的鮑伯坐在椅子上沉思了一會兒，靜了靜心情。他親了親那張小臉，終於接受那無可挽回的事實，懷著愉悅的心情下樓。

全家人圍在壁爐旁談天，母女仍做著針線活。鮑伯跟大家說史古基的外甥人很好意，儘管以前只見過一次面，今天在街上遇到，他看鮑伯有點兒——「就是有點兒心情不好」，於是便問鮑伯發生了什麼憂心的事。

鮑伯說：「他是說話最和氣的紳士，經他這麼一問，我就把家裡發生的事全告訴了他了。他說：『克瑞奇先生，很難過發生這樣的事情，由衷請您和您的好太太節哀。』只是，他怎麼會知道？這我就不清楚了。」

「知道什麼，親愛的？」

P. 180 「知道你是個好太太啊。」鮑伯答。

「這是大家都知道的事！」彼得說。

「說得好，兒子！」鮑伯大聲說：「希望大家都知道。他又說，『由衷請您的好太太節哀，要是有什麼我能幫得上忙的地方，』他把名片遞給我：『我就住這裡，請一定要來找我。』」鮑伯大聲說道：「倒不是因為他能幫上我們什麼忙，而是他的好意讓人很感動，好像他真的認識我們的小提姆，跟我們一樣很難過。」

「他一定是個好心人。」克瑞奇太太說。

「親愛的，要是你見過他、跟他說過話，你會更確定他是個好人。我說啊，要是他幫彼得找到更好的工作，我一點都不訝異。」鮑伯答道。

「彼得，你聽見了嗎？」克瑞奇太太說。

「那彼得就有伴了可以成家了。」一個女兒說道。

「別扯了！」彼得笑嘻嘻地反駁說。

「親愛的，雖然那還早得很，但說不一定總有一天會吧。但不管我們什麼時候分開，為了什麼分開，相信大家誰都不會忘了可憐的小提姆，他是第一個離開我們的，對吧？」鮑伯說道。

P. 181　　「永遠都不會忘記的，父親！」大家異口同聲說。

「而且我知道，在我們回想起雖然他只是個小小孩，卻那麼堅強那麼溫暖時，就不會隨便吵嘴而忘了可憐的小提姆。」鮑伯說。

「不會的，父親，永遠不會的！」他們異口同聲喊道。

「我很高興，很高興！」鮑伯說。

克瑞奇太太親了他一下，女兒親了他一下，兩個小鬼也親親他，彼得則和他握握手。小提姆，你的靈魂，你純真的本性就來自上帝的恩賜！

史古基說：「幽靈，不知怎的，我就是有預感我們分開的時刻快到了。告訴我吧，我們先前看到的那躺在床上的死者是誰？」

跟之前一樣，「來日聖誕幽靈」又帶他來商人聚集之地，不過他還是沒有找到自己的身影（不過時間不一樣了，他心想他們看到的這些未來影象似乎不分先後順序）。

幽靈沒有逗留片刻，只顧著往前飄去，好像要走到哪一個目的地。最後史古基只好央求他暫停一下腳步。

P. 182「我們現在匆忙經過的這個院落，是我工作的地方，我在那裡工作很久了。我看到那棟房子了，讓我看看我未來的樣子吧！」史古基說。

幽靈停下來了，手卻指著別的地方。

「房子在那邊，你為什麼指著別的方向？」史古基喊道。

幽靈的手還是指著同一個方向。

史古基急忙走到辦公室窗前往裡看了看。那還是一間辦公室，卻不是他的了，家具不一樣，坐在椅子上的人也不是他。幽靈依舊指著另一個方向。

他只好跟著幽靈走，心想自己怎麼不在那兒，到底去了哪裡。他跟幽靈一直走到一扇鐵門前才停下來，看了看四周才走進去。

　　這裡是教堂的墓園！他想去揭曉身分的那個可憐人已長眠地下了。真是個好地方，四面房屋環繞，雜草蔓延叢生。然而讓這些植物得以生長的並不是生命而是死亡。這裡擠滿了墳墓，土地吸足了養分，肥沃無比。真是個好地方！

P. 183　　幽靈站在一片墳墓之間，手向下指著一座墳墓。史古基渾身顫抖走過去。幽靈仍舊是先前的樣子，但是他卻害怕會從幽靈嚴肅的外表中讀出別的含意。

「在我走近你指的那座墳墓之前，你先回答我一個問題。」史古基說：「眼前的這些景像是將來『一定會』發生的事，還是只是『可能』發生的事？」

幽靈仍舊只是用手指著一旁的那座墳墓。

「一個人選擇什麼樣的路，就會走向什麼樣的終點。如果道路沒變，走向的終點自然一樣。但如果走出了原有的道路，終點就改變。這就是你要我明白的道理吧。」史古基說。

幽靈依然紋風不動。

史古基顫抖著慢慢走向那座墳墓。他順著幽靈的手指，看到被冷落的墓碑上刻著他自己的名字：耶柏尼澤‧史古基。

「剛才躺在床上的人，就是我？」他跪了下來，喊道。

幽靈的手從墳墓轉而指著他，又指回墳墓。

「不，幽靈！哦，不，不會的！」

幽靈的手仍指著墓碑。

P. 185　「幽靈啊！」他揪著幽靈的長袍哭喊道，「聽我說，我已經不是過去的我了。經歷了這些，我不再是原來的我了。我要是沒指望了，為什麼你要帶我來看這些呢？」

「不，幽靈！哦，不，不會的！」

幽靈的手終於動了一下。

「好心的幽靈啊，」他俯伏在幽靈面前，「求你慈悲的心憐憫我，替我求情。答應我，只要我重新做人，你給我看的那些景象就有可能改變。」

那隻仁慈的手開始顫抖了。

「我會打從心底去尊敬聖誕節，一整年都心存敬意。我會活在過去、現在、未來所見一切，牢牢記住三位幽靈，不會忘記你們給我的教訓。哦，請告訴我，我還有機會把墓碑上的字擦掉！」

痛苦不已的史古基抓住幽靈的手。幽靈想把手抽出來，但他苦苦哀求，緊抓不放。不過，幽靈的力氣更大，甩開了他的手。

史古基舉起雙手，最後一次哀求幽靈改變他的命運。此刻他看到幽靈的頭帽和長袍有了改變，幽靈縮小了，黑袍垮了下去，縮成了一根床柱。

第五樂章

曲終

P. 186　　沒錯！而且那正是他的床柱、他自己的床、房間也是他的。但最高興的是眼前的時間也是自己的，可以用來彌補過去！

　　「我會活出我的過去、現在、未來！」史古基滾下床不斷說道：「我會牢牢記住三位幽靈。哦，雅各・馬里啊！讚美上帝、讚美聖誕節！我是跪著說的，老雅各，我是跪著說的！」

　　他懷著行善之心，內心激動不已，神情容光煥發，嘶啞的聲音幾乎不聽使喚。先前他跟幽靈拉扯時曾痛哭流涕，臉上佈滿淚痕。

　　「床帳沒有被拆下來，」史古基大叫著，把一邊床帳抓在懷裡，「床帳、掛鉤，什麼都沒有被拆下來，東西都還在，我也還在，那些未來的景象是可以抹掉的，一定可以，我知道一定可以的！」

P. 187　　他的雙手把身上衣服扯來扯去，把內裡翻出來顛

倒著穿。一手扯、一手扔，和衣服同歡。

「要怎麼辦才好啊！」史古基又哭又笑地叫嚷著，還把長筒襪纏在自己身上，扮起了希臘神話人物拉奧孔[1]：「我像羽毛一樣輕飄飄的，像天使一樣快樂，小學生一樣開心，又像醉漢一樣昏頭昏腦。祝大家聖誕快樂！祝全世界新年快樂！喂，呀呼！哈囉！」

P.188 他雀躍地來到客廳，氣喘吁吁地站在那裡。

---

1 希臘神話人物，為特洛伊城的祭司，因警告特洛伊人勿中木馬計而觸怒天神，之後與兩個兒子遭海中巨蟒纏死。

史古基大叫：「那是裝燕麥粥的鍋子！」他圍著壁爐跳來跳去。「那是雅各‧馬里的鬼魂飄進來的門！今日聖誕幽靈就是坐在這個角落！那是我看見鬼魂飄盪的窗戶！現在沒事了，那些事都是真的，真的發生過。哈，哈，哈！」

說真的，一個這麼多年沒有開口笑的人，這一笑可燦爛了，非常動人，更引發了一長串燦爛的笑！

「我不知道今天是幾號，也不知道和幽靈在一起多久了，我什麼都不知道，就像剛出生的嬰兒一樣，不管了，無所謂，我寧可當個新生兒。哈囉！喔！呀呼！」史古基說道。

這時教堂傳來從未聽過的響亮鐘聲，打斷了他興奮的歡呼聲。鐘發出的撞擊聲，報時的噹噹聲，音錘敲打的叮噹聲，叮，噹，叮叮噹噹！哦，太美妙了，太美妙了！

P. 189 他衝到窗戶邊，打開窗戶，把頭探出去。沒有濃霧，沒有薄靄，天氣晴朗明媚，一派歡樂、熱鬧。氣溫很低，冷到要呼喚著血液跳起舞來了。金色陽光、美麗天空、清甜空氣、悅耳鐘聲。哦，太美好了，太美好了！

「今天是什麼日子啊？」史古基對著樓下盛裝的

小男孩喊道，那男孩他大概是閒晃進來看他怎麼了。

「啊？」男孩吃驚地答道。

「好孩子，今天是什麼日子呀？」史古基說。

「今天？就聖誕節呀！」男孩答道。

「今天是聖誕節！」史古基自言自語道，「我還沒有錯過聖誕節！三位幽靈一個晚上就把所有事都給辦完了，幽靈可以隨意自如，當然可以，當然可以啦。哈囉，好孩子！」

「哈囉！」男孩回答。

「你知道隔壁街轉角那間賣雞鴨的店嗎？」史古基問。

「知道呀。」小男孩答道。

「真是聰明的孩子！好棒！那你知道掛在上面的那隻上等火雞賣了沒有？不是小隻的，是大的那隻。」史古基說。

P. 191　「你是說跟我差不多大的那隻嗎？」男孩答道。

「真是個可愛的孩子！跟他說話真有趣。沒錯，小鬼！」史古基說。

「現在還掛在那裡。」小男孩說。

「還在嗎？去幫我買下來吧。」史古基說。

「你在說笑吧！」小男孩喊道。

「不，不，我是說真的。去把牠買下來，叫他們送過來這裡，我再跟他們說要送到哪裡去。你跟送貨的人一起過來，我就給你一先令。要是你們能在五分鐘內過來，我就給你半克朗！」史古基說。

　　男孩飛也似地跑開。槍手扣扳機的手可要夠穩，他的射靶速度才能有男孩的一半快。

　　「我要把火雞送給鮑伯・克瑞奇那一家人！」史古基搓著雙手，喃喃自語，笑了起來。「他一定不會知道是誰送的。那隻火雞有小提姆的兩倍大。把火雞送到鮑伯家，連喬・米勒[2]都從來沒有開過這樣的玩笑！」

P. 192　　他寫地址時手在發抖，不過還是寫好了，他走下樓開門等雞鴨店的送貨員到來。他站在那裡等待，門環吸引了他的目光。

　　「只要我活著一天，我就會好好愛護這個門環！」史古基用手輕輕拍著門環說道：「我以前都還沒有正眼瞧過門環，上面那張臉的表情多誠懇啊！真是個好門環！哦，火雞來了。哈囉！喔，你好！聖誕快樂！」

2　Joe Miller（1684–1738），英國十八世紀的知名喜劇演員。1739年，John Mottley 假這位喜劇演員之名，編輯了一本笑話集，後來引申用來比喻老掉牙的笑話。

「哦，火雞來了。哈囉！喔，你好！聖誕快樂！」

It was a Turkey!

這真的是一隻火雞！那火雞可真大，靠那兩隻腳一定站不起來，站一下腳就會像封蠟棒一樣啪地一聲折斷。

「哎呀，就這樣送不了肯頓城的，一定得叫輛馬車。」史古基說。

他咯咯笑說著。他付了火雞的錢，付了出租馬車的錢，給了男孩酬勞，還是一直咯咯笑個不停。坐下來時笑得更厲害了，笑到快喘不過氣來，噴出了眼淚。

因為他的手一直抖個不停，想要好好刮個鬍子都很難。就算沒有邊刮鬍子邊跳舞，也得專心才行。但就算把鼻尖削掉了一塊，他也只會心滿意足地貼上膠布了事。

P. 195　史古基穿上最好的衣服，終於來到了街上。這時街頭人潮湧現，一如今日聖誕幽靈帶他一起看過的街景。他一路手擱身後走著，笑逐顏開地看著每一個人。

總之，他看起來是那麼快樂洋溢，有三、四個和善的路人對他說：「早安，先生。祝您聖誕快樂！」史古基事後常說，在他聽來，這是他一生中聽過最愉快的聲音了。

沒走多遠，他看到一位福態的紳士迎面而來，是那個昨天去他辦公室說「我想這裡就是『史古基與馬里』

他一路上背著雙手，笑逐顏開地看著每一個人。

吧」的那位。一想到兩人撞見時，這位老紳士不知會鄙
視他，史古基心裡就一扎。不過他知道自己該怎麼做
了，於是走上前去。

「親愛的先生，」史古基加快腳步，雙手握住
老紳士的手，說道，「您好，希望您昨天的募款很順
利。您真是個好心人，祝您聖誕快樂，先生！」

P. 197 「史古基先生？」

「不錯，就是我本人，恐怕你聽到這名字會不太
開心。容我請求您的寬恕，您願不願意好心……」說到
這裡，史古基在他耳邊低聲說了幾句話。

「上帝保佑！親愛的史古基先生，您是說真的
嗎？」老紳士激動得快說不出話來。

「您要是同意的話，一分錢不少。其中一大筆
錢是早就該捐的，我保證一定會給，您能幫我這個忙
嗎？」史古基說。

老紳士握著史古基的雙手，說道：「哦，我親愛
的先生，不知道該怎麼說才好，你這麼慷……」史古基
打斷他的話，「請什麼都不用說，來看看我吧。您會來
找我嗎？」

老紳士大聲說道：「那當然了！」很顯然他一定
會去。

「謝謝您，非常感恩，不勝感激。上帝保佑您！」史古基說。

　　他去了教堂，也在街上逛了逛，看著來往匆匆的行人。他輕輕拍拍孩子們的頭，問候乞丐，往下看了看人家的廚房，抬頭望了望窗戶，發現每樣東西都那麼有趣。他以前做夢也沒想到，只是散散步，什麼事情都可以帶給他這麼多的快樂。到了下午，他轉身往外甥家走去。

P. 198　　他在門口來回徘徊了十幾次，最後才鼓起勇氣，一鼓作氣衝上去敲門。

　　史古基對小女孩說：「你家主人在嗎？」那女孩可真可愛！

　　「他在，先生。」

　　「他人在哪裡呢？」史古基說。

　　「先生，他在飯廳裡，和太太在一起。我可以帶您上樓。」

　　史古基說，「謝謝你，他認識我的。」這時他的手已經握住飯廳的門把，「我從這裡進去。」

　　他輕輕轉動門把，側著臉往門邊探頭進去。裡面的人正看著桌上擺得滿滿的菜，因為年輕家庭主婦在這方面總是容易神經緊張，喜歡看到樣樣事情都安排穩妥。

「是我，你的舅舅史古基。我來圍爐了，
　你願不願意讓我加入，弗瑞德？」

「弗瑞德！」史古基喊道。

P. 199　天啊！外甥媳吃了好大一驚。史古基一時忘了她坐在屋角的腳凳上，不然他無論如何也不會那樣叫喊。

「哦，我的天啊！看看是誰來了？」弗瑞德喊道。

「是我，你的舅舅史古基。我來吃晚餐了，你願不願意讓我加入，弗瑞德？」

快進來吧！謝天謝地，還好弗瑞德沒有把自己的胳膊給揮斷了。不一會兒，他就像在自己家裡那樣熱絡起來了。外甥媳模樣依舊，托普、豐腴妹妹，還有其他人，大家陸續到來，每個人看起來都沒變。美好的餐宴，美好的遊戲，一切都是那麼美好，那麼和諧，歡樂不已！

隔天他早早就到了辦公室。哦，真的是一大早就到了。他心裡正盤算著，他要早一點到才能逮到鮑伯·克瑞奇遲到！

他成功了，他的確先到了！時鐘敲響了九點，沒見到鮑伯。一刻鐘過去了，還是不見鮑伯人影，他整整遲到了十八分鐘半。史古基把門敞開坐著，這樣才看得到他走進他的「櫃子」。

鮑伯還沒開門就先脫下帽子、拿下圍巾，飛快地坐到他的小凳子上提筆疾書，彷彿要把遲到的時間給補回來。

P. 201　　「嘿！你這個時候才來上班，是什麼意思？」史古基咆哮著，盡量裝出平時說話的語調。

　　「真的很抱歉，先生，我遲到了。」鮑伯說。

　　「你遲到了？」史古基重複他的話。「沒錯，你遲到了。麻煩你給我過來這裡一下。」

　　「一年就這麼一次了，先生，以後再也不會了。」

　　鮑伯從「櫃子」裡走出來懇求道：「我昨天玩得太開心了點，先生。」

　　「現在，我要說啊，朋友，」史古基說，「我不想再忍受這種事情了，所以……」史古基說著從凳子上跳起來，手指用力往鮑伯的背心上一戳，鮑伯踉踉蹌蹌地退回「櫃子」裡去，「所以，我要給你加薪！」

　　鮑伯嚇得打哆嗦，身子稍稍靠近了一把尺。他突然冒出個念頭，想用尺把史古基敲昏，抓住他，然後叫巷子裡的人帶件瘋子穿的緊身衣過來幫忙。

　　「聖誕快樂，鮑伯！」史古基一臉真誠，不可能搞錯。他拍拍鮑伯的背說道：「聖誕快樂，鮑伯，我的好夥伴！祝你有個更愉快的聖誕節，這麼多年來我早就該給你的！我要給你加薪，還要努力幫助你辛苦的家人。鮑伯，今天下午我們就一邊喝著熱騰騰的果子

「我要給你加薪！」

「我要給你加薪！」

酒，一邊討論你的事吧！鮑伯‧克瑞奇，把爐火升起來吧，先去買桶煤炭，再來做好工作吧！」

P. 203　　史古基說到做到，而且做的比說的多。小提姆沒有死，他還成了小提姆的第二個爸爸。他變成了這樣一個好朋友、好老闆、好人，不管是倫敦這個美好的古城，或是這個美好的古老世界上，大大小小的各個美好的古老地方，都不曾見過像他這樣的人。

　　有人嘲笑他的轉變，但是他任由人們取笑，不去搭理。他夠聰明的，知道世上不論什麼事情起初一定會受到世人嘲笑。他知道這些人只是不明就裡，反正人們能夠常常瞇著眼睛、咧嘴笑，疾病就比較不會橫行。他自己心裡開心，這對他來說就夠了。

P. 205　　自此以後，他沒有再和幽靈打過交道，生活上嚴守滴酒不沾[3]的原則。大家一提到史古基，都會說他是世上最懂得怎麼過聖誕節的人。但願我們每個人也是如此，人人都懂得怎麼過聖誕節！最後，套句小提姆說的話：願上帝保佑我們每一個人！

3　spirit 有「幽靈」之意，也有「酒精」之意。「不和幽靈打交道」和「不沾染酒精」有雙關語的趣味。

小氣財神
A CHRISTMAS CAROL

作者 _ 狄更斯（Charles Dickens）

插圖 _ A. C. Michael, A. I. Keller, Arthur Rackham
C. E. Brock, E. A. Abbey, Fred Barnard
G. A. Williams, Harold Copping, Harry Furniss
John Leech, John R. Neill, Roberta Paflin
S. J. Willcox, Sol Eytinge

譯者 _ 楊舒評

校對 _ 黃詩韻

編輯 _ 安卡斯

封面設計 _ 林書玉

製程管理 _ 洪巧玲

發行人 _ 周均亮

出版者 _ 寂天文化事業股份有限公司

電話 _ +886-2-2365-9739

傳真 _ +886-2-2365-9835

網址 _ www.icosmos.com.tw

讀者服務 _ onlineservice@icosmos.com.tw

出版日期 _ 2018年12月 初版三刷（250101）

郵撥帳號 _ 1998620-0 寂天文化事業股份有限公司

國家圖書館出版品預行編目資料

小氣財神（原著雙語彩圖本）/ 狄更斯（Charles
Dickens）著；楊舒評 譯. —初版. —[臺北市]：
寂天文化, 2018.12 面；公分. 中英對照;
譯自：A Christmas Carol

ISBN　978-986-318-720-2 (25K平裝)

873.59　　　　　　　　　　　　107012184